KU-734-917

This type of gun was developed in the late 1300's. As it could be depressed more than forty-five degrees, it was used for defending the battlements of castles. The diameter of the cannon ball it fired was about two inches.

THE GUNS

Developed in Germany in the fifteenth century, this gun had five barrels which were fired one at a time. Although of fairly small calibre, the speed with which it could be fired made this a useful weapon.

THE VICTOR
BOOK FOR BOYS 1971

CONTENTS

Printed and Published in Great Britain by D. C. Thomson & Co., Ltd., Dundee and London.

© D. C. THOMSON & CO., LTD., 1970.

THE BATTLE FOR THE BRIDGES

It was the night of June 5th, 1944, during the Second World War, and the men of the 2nd Battalion, The Oxford and Buckinghamshire Light Infantry, 5th Parachute Brigade, were going aboard their gliders. The next day was D-Day, the day when a combined British and American force would invade German-occupied France. But even before this combined force set out, the glider troops would be in action. Their orders were to capture and hold the bridges over the Caen Canal and the River Orne until the invading troops arrived.

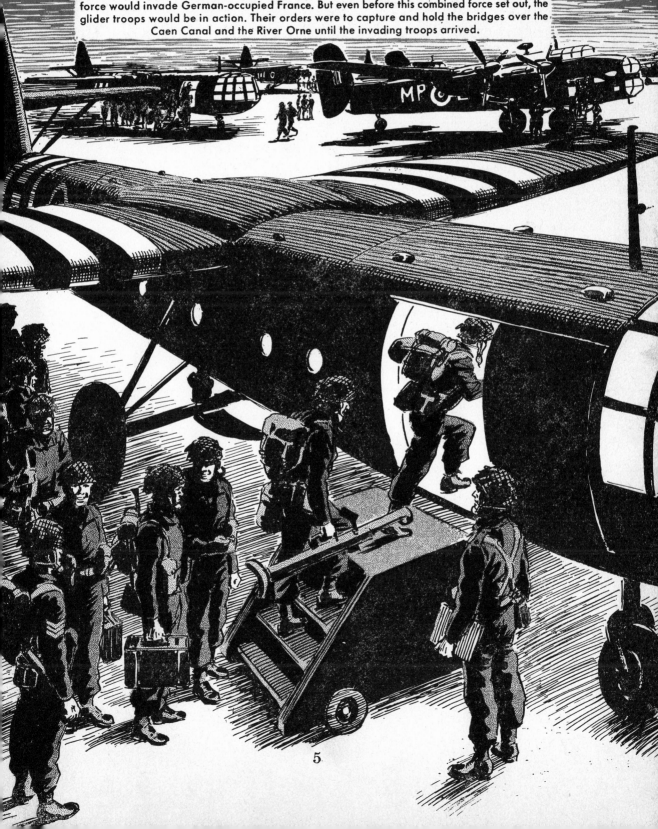

"Brace yourselves for the landing."

WELL, THIS IS IT, WALLY. A FREE TRIP TO FRANCE!

LET'S HOPE WE'VE GOT RETURN TICKETS, BILL!

GOOD LUCK, LADS!

AYE, THEY'LL BE NEEDING IT, I'M THINKING, JAMIE!

The crossing was uneventful. Heavy raids by the R.A.F. on enemy installations claimed the full attention of the German fighter aircraft and anti-aircraft batteries.

As soon as the French coast was crossed, when D-Day was only nine minutes old, the gliders cast off from their towing planes. Silently, they swooped towards their objectives.

BANG ON, TIM! WE SHAN'T BE MORE THAN 50 YARDS FROM OUR BRIDGE!

ROGER! TELL 'EM TO CARRY OUT LANDING DRILL!

THIS IS IT! LINK ARMS! BRACE YOURSELVES FOR THE LANDING!

HIMMEL! A GLIDER!

ENGLANDERS! ACHTUNG! ACHTUNG!

6

"Forward the Ox and Bucks!"

Three gliders crash-landed near the eastern end of the canal bridge, whilst the other three flew on and landed at the western end of the bridge over the River Orne.

FORWARD, THE OX AND BUCKS! CHARGE!

AAARGH!

CAFE DU NORD

GET ACROSS! SECURE THE OTHER END OF THE BRIDGE!

AARGH!

AARGH!

A MACHINE-GUN! WATCH OUT!

GRENADE GOING OVER! MIND YOUR HEADS!

GOOD SHOT, WALKER!

Meanwhile, other troops and the pilots were unloading the heavier weapons from the glider.

HERE YOU ARE, LADS—MORTARS AND PIAT ANTI-TANK GUNS!

7

"Where the dickens are we, Joe?"

So far, everything had gone according to plan, but the good luck which had favoured the glider-borne troops did not last for the 7th Battalian, who arrived by parachute. A wind sprang up and scattered them as they came down.

Fortunately, the commanding officer had come prepared. No sooner had he landed than he began to blow the regimental call on a bugle.

"Blimey! Somebody's gunning for us!"

HERE HE IS! HE MUST HAVE LEATHER LUNGS—I HEARD HIM A MILE OFF!

HA, HA! YOU'D HAVE HEARD HIM TEN MILES OFF IF HE'D BLOWN THE COOKHOUSE CALL, DINGER!

The bugle calls made things easier for Walker and Mayes as well.

I KNOW THAT CALL. IT'S THE REGIMENTAL CALL OF THE 7TH PARATROOPS!

COME ON THEN. LET'S FIND THE GEEZER WHO'S DOING ALL THE BLOWING!

HI! WHAT'S BEEN KEEPING YOU BLOKES—AND WHO'S MAKING THAT 'ORRIBLE NOISE?

THAT'S OUR C.O., MATE, AND YOU BETTER BE CAREFUL HE DON'T HEAR YOU. HE'S PROUD OF HIS BUGLING!

WE'RE FROM THE 2ND OX AND BUCKS, SIR. BOTH BRIDGES HAVE BEEN TAKEN AND WE WERE SENT TO ACT AS GUIDES.

FIRST RATE SHOW! I'VE ONLY MANAGED TO COLLECT ABOUT 200 MEN BUT YOU CAN MOVE OFF RIGHT AWAY. WE CAN'T AFFORD TO WAIT ANY LONGER.

With the arrival of the 7th Parachute Battalion, an area including the two bridges was sealed off and defensive positions established. Walker and Mayes reported back to their own unit and preparations were made to meet the heavy German counter-attacks which everyone knew would inevitably be launched. They hadn't long to wait!

BLIMEY! SOMEBODY'S GUNNING FOR US!

THAT'S HEAVY STUFF. KEEP YOUR HEADS DOWN!

SARGE! LOOK! THEY'VE BROUGHT UP THEIR PERISHING NAVY!

STRIKE A LIGHT! IT'S A GERMAN GUN-BOAT!

WALKER, GET BACK TO THE MAJOR AND TELL HIM THE SITUATION. ASK HIM TO SEND UP A PIAT TEAM—AND FOR THE LOVE OF MIKE GET A MOVE ON!

"Everybody keep down till she gets a bit closer!"

WHAT A LIFE! I JOIN AN AIRBORNE UNIT AND END UP FIGHTING THE GERMAN NAVY!

A GUN-BOAT? THAT'S ALL WE NEEDED! WHERE'S THAT BLOOMING PIAT?

WE SENT THE PIAT ALONG THE CANAL TOWARDS CAEN, SIR. THERE'S SUPPOSED TO BE A GUN-BOAT ATTACKING FROM THAT DIRECTION!

ANOTHER? BLIMEY, WE'VE GOT ONE OF THEM ON OUR FLANK, TOO!

YOU'LL HAVE TO DO THE BEST YOU CAN, WALKER. TELL YOUR PLATOON COMMANDER I'LL SEND HIM HEAVY WEAPONS AS SOON AS I POSSIBLY CAN!

Walker reported back to his sergeant.

WHERE'S THE PIAT THEN?

WE AIN'T THE ONLY ONES WITH GUN-BOAT TROUBLE, SARGE. THE PIAT IS ALREADY IN ACTION.

MAYBE WE COULD DO SOMETHING WITH THIS GAMMON BOMB, SARGE.

WE'D NEVER CHUCK A GAMMON BOMB FAR ENOUGH.

I RECKON I CAN, WALLY. EVERYBODY KEEP DOWN TILL SHE GETS A BIT CLOSER!

ANOTHER COUPLE OF MINUTES SHOULD DO IT!

NOW FOR IT!

HIMMEL! THERE IS ONE OF THEM! SHOOT HIM!

12

"Fix bayonets!

GOOD SHOW, WALKER!

I KNEW YOU WERE GOOD AT HURLING THE DISCUS, BILL, BUT I WOULD NEVER HAVE THOUGHT YOU COULD HAVE HURLED THAT GAMMON BOMB HARD ENOUGH TO MAKE IT BOUNCE ON THE WATER LIKE IT DID.

With a gaping hole blown in her bows, the gun-boat filled and sank quickly.

The gun-boat attacking on the other flank had even less luck. A direct hit by a PIAT projectile struck her amidships and blew up her ammunition.

That was the end of the German Navy's attempt to intervene in the battle, but all through the morning the troops had to beat off determined counter-attacks. The main landings of the invasion force were now taking place on the Normandy beaches, but still the Germans mustered more troops, tanks and guns for another attack on the British airborne forces. The first thrust was on the village of Benouville, held by A Company of the Paratroopers. But it so happened that A Company had had a stroke of good luck.

CRUMBS! A GERMAN ANTI-TANK GUN AND THEY'VE GOT A PUNCTURE!

IT'S ALMOST A SHAME TO CLOBBER THE POOR PERISHERS—

WE AIN'T GOING TO— NOT TILL THEY'VE CHANGED THE WHEEL ANYWAY!

WELL, THEY TOOK THEIR TIME BUT THEY'VE FINISHED AT LAST!

YES, AND NOW WE'LL DO OUR STUFF! FIX BAYONETS, YOU BLOODTHIRSTY LOT!

The Germans counter attack!

Meanwhile, the Germans were about to launch their assault.

14.

THE WINNER CAME IN EIGHTH!

Alf Tupper, the runner known as the Tough of the Track, was one of Britain's best middle-distance runners, but during the winter he ran in cross-country races to keep himself in trim. Now he was running in a race, the first twenty finishers of which would qualify to run in the Highcliffe Cup, an important international event, the following Saturday.

I'M GETTING LEFT TOO FAR BEHIND HERE. I'D BETTER MOVE UP A BIT.

THAT'S BETTER! I'M WITHIN STRIKING DISTANCE OF THE LEADERS NOW.

ZAT ONE! NUMBAIRE FIVE! HE IS TUPPAIRE, ZE WELL KNOWN RUNNER.

OUI, PIERRE! BUT HE IS ZE TRACK MAN! NOT A CROSS-COUNTRY RUNNER.

START OF

START

LAST TIME ROUND! LAST TIME ROUND!

Alf improved his position throughout the last lap, then with half a mile to go—

NOW FOR IT! IF I GET IN FRONT NOW I SHOULD BE ABLE TO HOLD THEM OFF.

I CAN'T LET ALF GET TOO FAR IN FRONT OR I'LL NEVER HAVE A HOPE OF CATCHING HIM.

ROBSON'S CATCHING UP ON TUPPER!

AYE, BUT HE WON'T BEAT HIM. ALF WAS CRAFTY ENOUGH TO GRAB A LEAD WHEN IT MATTERED.

TUPPER WINS!

ZAT TUPPAIRE—HE MUST BE WATCHED. HE IS ZE GOOD CROSS-COUNTRY RUNNER ALSO, PIERRE.

WELL DONE, ALF!

OUI, LOUIS, WE MUST WARN MARCEL ABOUT ZAT ONE! HE MAY WANT TO ARRANGE SOMETHING FOR HIM.

Pierre and Louis were spies for Marcel Moreau, a well-known French cross-country runner, who had entered for the Highcliffe Cup. Moreau and his father owned a gambling club in Paris and had bet a large amount of money that he would win the cup. When they arrived in Britain on the Tuesday, Pierre and Louis reported to them at Moreau's training quarters—

WELL, WHAT DID YOU FIND OUT?

THERE ARE ONLY TWO WORTH BOTHERING ABOUT. ONE EES ALFRED TUPPAIRE, ZE FAMOUS RUNNER, AND ZE OTHER EES CALLED TOM ROBSON.

ROBSON YOU HAVE NOT TO WORRY ABOUT SO MUCH BUT ZAT TUPPAIRE, HE IS VERY CRAFTY, VERY CRAFTY INDEED.

18

Alf is kidnapped!

"This'll keep you quiet."

Alf soon got on to the main road, but—

"A week tied up and he runs like ze demon!"

CHANGING TENT

I'VE MADE IT IN TIME. I COULD JUST GO AND TELL ABOUT MOREAU AND GET HIM THROWN OUT—BUT THAT AIN'T MY WAY OF DOING THINGS. I'LL BEAT HIM IN THE RACE SOMEHOW AND FINISH HIM AND HIS CROOKED BETTING THAT WAY.

The runners lined up for the start of the race.

THERE'S THAT RAT MOREAU! I'LL HAVE TO SET A FAST PACE AND SEE IF I CAN BREAK HIM.

SACRE BLEU! TUPPAIRE! HOW DID HE GET HERE? STILL I WILL BEAT HIM EASILY. HE HAS BEEN TIED FOR ZE WEEK. THEN EET IS JUST HEES WORD AGAINST MINE AS TO WHAT HAPPENED. I HAVE NOTHINGS TO WORRY ABOUT.

INTERNATIONAL CROSS-COUNTRY RACE

LOOK AT TUPPER! HE'S SETTING FAR TOO FAST A PACE.

NOM D'UN NOM! LOOK AT ZAT TUPPAIRE! HE STILL RUNS FAST. ONE NEVER KNOWS WITH HEEM. I WILL HAVE TO GO AFTER HEEM!

RACE

At the end of the first lap—

YOU'RE WELL IN FRONT, ALF, BUT THAT FRENCHMAN, MOREAU, IS AFTER YOU.

GOOD, HE'S FALLEN FOR IT. I JUST HOPE I CAN KEEP THIS UP TILL HE BREAKS.

HE STILL RUNS ON, ZAT ONE! HE EES NOT HUMAN! A WEEK TIED UP AND HE RUNS LIKE ZE DEMON! I WEEL NEVER CATCH HIM.

23

THE THIEF OF TWALA

Jim Cameron, an engineer, had been many weeks in Twala, in the Sudanese Desert, engaged in driving a well near a dried-up oasis. Now shortly before dawn one day he suddenly wakened up. He lay still for a moment collecting his thoughts.

WHAT'S HAPPENING? MY WATCH—WHERE'S IT GONE?

GOT YOU! SO YOU THOUGHT YOU'D HAVE MY WATCH DID YOU? WELL THAT WATCH IS PRECIOUS TO ME. I'M GOING TO TAKE YOU TO EL BABA, THE CHIEF OF THE TRIBE, AND YOU CAN ANSWER TO HIM FOR YOUR THEFT.

I'VE HAD A FEW THINGS STOLEN FROM ME RECENTLY BUT NOW AT LAST I'VE CAUGHT YOU AND I MEAN TO SEE YOU PUNISHED.

CHIEF, I FOUND THIS LOW DOG ATTEMPTING TO STEAL MY WATCH WHILE I WAS ASLEEP. I BRING HIM TO YOU FOR PUNISHMENT.

A THOUSAND TIMES HAS THIS FELLOW BEEN WHIPPED BUT STILL HE HAS NO RESPECT FOR THE LAW OF THE TRIBE. IT SEEMS I HAVE BEEN TOO LENIENT WITH HIM. I WILL SPEAK MORE WITH YOU SCOUTS LATER.

"Perhaps soon blood will flow into the well."

HO, THERE, YOU TWO OF MY BODY-GUARD! OVER HERE! TAKE THIS DOG AND CUT OFF THE HAND WHICH TRIED TO STEAL THE WATCH OF THE STRANGER. THEN TURN HIM LOOSE INTO THE DESERT.

STOP!

STOP THIS, CHIEF! NO MAN SHALL BE CRIPPLED SIMPLY FOR STEALING MY WATCH.

BUT THE THIEF MUST BE PUNISHED AND IT IS THE LAW OF THE TRIBE THAT HE SHOULD LOSE HIS HAND.

EL BABA, I NEED A SERVANT AND YOU TOLD ME THAT YOU WOULD FIND A MAN WHO COULD BE TRUSTED. NOW I WILL TAKE THIS THIEF FOR HE HAS BEEN SO BADLY FRIGHTENED THAT HE WILL NOT TRY TO STEAL AGAIN.

THAT IS WISE. YOU MAY HAVE THIS THIEF FOR A SERVANT BUT IF HE STEALS ONE MORE THING HE WILL LOSE HIS HAND AND PERHAPS HIS HEAD!

STAY WITH ME A LITTLE AND TELL ME HOW YOUR WELL IS GOING. HAVE YOU FOUND WATER YET?

NOT YET, ALTHOUGH I'VE GONE DOWN NEARLY FOUR HUNDRED FEET AND NOW I HAVE COME TO DRY SAND AGAIN. BUT I AM SURE THAT THERE IS WATER THERE—MY INSTRUMENTS TELL ME IT IS THERE.

PERHAPS SOON BLOOD WILL FLOW INTO THE WELL IN PLACE OF WATER. MY SCOUTS BRING ME BAD NEWS. EVERYWHERE THE SPRINGS HAVE DRIED UP AND MANY TRIBES ARE DYING OF THIRST. THERE IS NO WATER IN ALL THE DESERT EXCEPT IN THE BIG TANK WHICH WE HAVE BUILT IN THIS OASIS.

WITH CARE YOU MIGHT MAKE THE WATER LAST UNTIL THE RAINS COME. I MEASURED THE WATER IN THE TANK WHEN I FIRST ARRIVED. BY NOW YOU SHOULD STILL HAVE OVER A HUNDRED GALLONS.

THAT IS TRUE. BUT THERE IS NOT ENOUGH WATER TO SHARE AND I HAVE HAD TO SEND BACK MESSENGERS FROM THE SENUSSI TRIBE TELLING THEM SO. NOW I HEAR THAT THE THIRST IS SO GREAT THAT THE SENUSSI ARE COMING TO TAKE OUR WATER BY FORCE. THAT IS WHY MY MEN ARE DEPLOYED ALL ROUND THIS OASIS.

BUT THE SENUSSI ARE A POWERFUL TRIBE AND THIS COULD DEVELOP INTO A REAL WAR.

Still no water!

I SEE THE TRIBE IS DEPLOYED TO REPEL AN ATTACK. IF I CAN FIND WATER THERE WON'T BE ANY WAR. I'LL HAVE TO START WORK RIGHT AWAY—THERE ISN'T A MOMENT TO LOSE.

THERE IS WATER NEAR THE BOTTOM OF THE SHAFT I'VE BORED AND I WILL DO ALL I CAN TO GET THROUGH TO IT. IF I DO, THERE WILL BE ENOUGH WATER FOR YOUR PEOPLE AND THE SENUSSI AS WELL. NOW I MUST BE OFF. IT MAY TAKE ME SOME TIME.

FAREWELL FOR NOW. I HOPE YOU FIND THE WATER.

Cameron went back to his tent first and there he found Klib awaiting him.

LORD, MAY I PRESENT THIS GIFT TO YOU IN GRATITUDE FOR SAVING MY LIFE?

I'VE SEEN THAT THING BEFORE—WHY IT'S EL BABA'S! YOU MUST HAVE STOLEN THAT EVEN WHILE HE WAS ORDERING YOUR HAND TO BE CUT OFF.

I DID NOT STEAL IT, LORD. TRULY IT FELL INTO MY HAND.

YOU BLOOMING PICKPOCKET. STILL I'VE NO TIME TO PUT OFF. I HAVE MUCH WORK TO DO IF BLOODSHED IS TO BE AVOIDED.

Suddenly—

A SHOT! IT MUST BE THE SENUSSI! IT LOOKS AS IF THERE'S GOING TO BE A BATTLE BEFORE I CAN EVEN GET STARTED.

IT'S THE SENUSSI ALL RIGHT BUT EL BABA'S MEN HAVE GIVEN THEM SOMETHING TO THINK ABOUT. MY GUESS IS THEY EXPECTED TO TAKE THE OASIS BY SURPRISE. AND NOW THAT'S GONE THEY WILL HAVE TO THINK OF NEW PLANS. THAT SHOULD GIVE ME AT LEAST A FEW HOURS OF PEACE! I'VE JUST GOT TO GET WATER INTO MY WELL!

Cameron wasted no time in getting to work and soon he had drilled another twenty feet down. At that point, he sent his native helpers down the well to bring up a sample of the ground the drill was boring through. But when they reached the top, Cameron was disappointed to find it was still fine, dry sand. Cameron then fitted the last section of drill he had and started drilling again.

Some minutes later—

DRILL MAKES FUNNY NOISE, BOSS.

WE'VE DRILLED TO THE END OF OUR LAST SECTION OF DRILL. WE CAN GO NO DEEPER. THE NOISE IS THE DRILL RATTLING ROUND AND ROUND IN THE HOLE IT HAS ALREADY BORED. STOP THE ENGINE, BOYS, AND WE'LL HAUL UP THE DRILL.

"I will kill you rather than go down that well!"

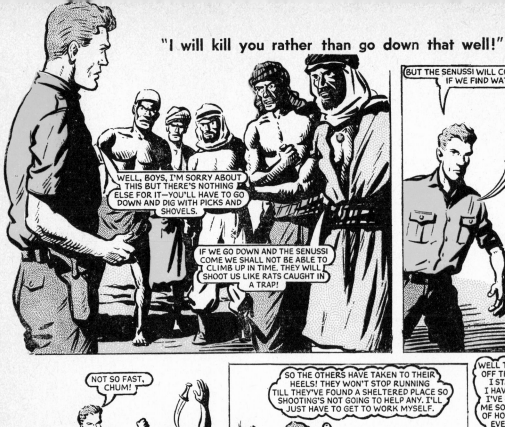

WELL, BOYS, I'M SORRY ABOUT THIS BUT THERE'S NOTHING ELSE FOR IT—YOU'LL HAVE TO GO DOWN AND DIG WITH PICKS AND SHOVELS.

IF WE GO DOWN AND THE SENUSSI COME WE SHALL NOT BE ABLE TO CLIMB UP IN TIME. THEY WILL SHOOT US LIKE RATS CAUGHT IN A TRAP!

BUT THE SENUSSI WILL COME IN PEACE IF WE FIND WATER!

I WILL KILL YOU RATHER THAN GO DOWN THAT WELL!

NOT SO FAST, CHUM!

SO THE OTHERS HAVE TAKEN TO THEIR HEELS! THEY WON'T STOP RUNNING TILL THEY'VE FOUND A SHELTERED PLACE SO SHOOTING'S NOT GOING TO HELP ANY. I'LL JUST HAVE TO GET TO WORK MYSELF.

WELL THERE'S NO POINT IN PUTTING OFF THE EVIL HOUR—THE QUICKER I START THE BETTER CHANCE I HAVE OF AVOIDING BLOODSHED. I'VE GOT MY INSTRUMENT WITH ME SO IT'LL GIVE ME A ROUGH IDEA OF HOW FAR I'LL HAVE TO DIG—OR EVEN IF THERE'S ANY POINT IN DIGGING AT ALL.

IT'S CERTAINLY A WELL MADE WELL SO FAR, BUT I'LL HAVE A LOT TO ANSWER FOR IF I DON'T FIND WATER HERE.

MY INSTRUMENT SHOWS THAT THERE IS WATER NEAR, YET THE SAND IS BONE DRY.

"For that theft El Baba would have our heads."

THIS IS GOING TO BE SOME JOB—THE SAND'S SO DRY THAT IT RUNS BACK INTO THE HOLE ALMOST AS SOON AS I'VE TAKEN IT OUT.

Suddenly—

WHAT THE HECK! I'VE SUNK INTO THE FLOOR—IT MUST BE QUICKSAND!

QUICKSAND! BUT IT WILL SUCK UP ALL THE WATER THERE IS AROUND. IT'S JUST LIKE THE WICK ON AN OIL LAMP. IT HAS TO BE THOROUGHLY SOAKED BEFORE IT WILL DRAW OIL THROUGH IT. NOW IF ONLY I COULD SOAK THIS QUICKSAND WITH WATER—

I MUST CONVINCE EL BABA TO LET ME USE THE WATER IN HIS TANK. THAT'S THE ONLY CHANCE I HAVE OF GETTING THIS WELL DRAWING WATER. BUT THAT OLD BUZZARD OF A CHIEF WILL NEVER AGREE OR I'M A DUTCHMAN. JUDGING BY THE SOUNDS ABOVE THE FIGHTING HAS STARTED ALREADY.

THAT WAS MIGHTY CLOSE. IT MIGHT BE TRICKY GETTING OVER THE PARAPET—I'LL HAVE TO MAKE A DIVE FOR IT!

THESE TWO EVIL ONES TRIED TO GET NEAR THE WELL, LORD. I DEALT WITH THEM.

YOU HAVE DONE WELL, KLIB. NOW I HAVE A PROPOSITION TO PUT TO YOU.

YOU HAVE SAID THAT YOU WOULD NOT STEAL ANY MORE BUT WOULD YOU STEAL FOR ME?

ALLAH WOULD FORGIVE ME, LORD. NAME YOUR DESIRE.

ONE HUNDRED GALLONS OF WATER.

ONE HUNDRED GALLONS OF WATER! LORD, FOR THAT THEFT EL BABA WOULD HAVE OUR HEADS—OR PERHAPS STAKE US OUT TO DIE MORE SLOWLY.

29

AIEE! THE SHOOTING IS COMING FROM THE STRANGER'S WELL— IT IS NOT THE SENUSSI AT ALL!

BUT WHAT IS THIS? IT IS PIPE FROM OUR WATER TANK. THE WHITE STRANGER IS STEALING OUR WATER!

The word quickly passed among the Arabs of what was happening to the precious supply of water and more than fifty made a rush towards the parapet of the well. Cameron and Klib were quickly surrounded and word was sent to El Baba.

DOG! WHAT IS THIS EVIL THING THAT YOU HAVE DONE?

I NEEDED WATER TO MAKE MY WELL WORK AND I KNEW YOU WOULD NOT HAVE HEEDED ME IF I HAD ASKED FOR THE WATER, SO I STOLE IT. IF I HAVE BEEN WRONG AND NO WATER COMES THEN KILL ME—I WILL DESERVE TO DIE!

I AM JUST! THE WATER IS LOST BUT IF IT BRINGS WATER AS THIS MAN CLAIMS THEN THE RETURN IS GREATER THAN THE LOSS. IF IT DOES NOT THEN HE IS A THIEF AND FOR A THEFT AS GREAT AS THIS, HIS DEATH SHALL BE THAT OF THE STAKE. IF THERE IS NO WATER WITHIN THE HOUR HE SHALL DIE.

One hour later—

ONE HOUR HAS PASSED AND STILL NO WATER HAS COME FROM YOUR WELL. IT IS TIME FOR YOU TO DIE. MY GUARDS WILL SEE TO IT.

WELL, THIS IS IT! IT WAS A GAMBLE AND I'D DO IT AGAIN IF I HAD TO.

31

Just then—

THE END

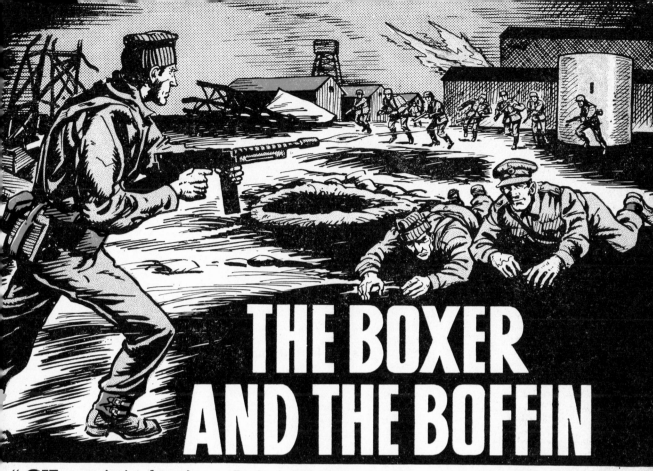

THE BOXER AND THE BOFFIN

"GET moving! At the double!"

Sergeant-Major Bowler roared at the squad of men who came scuttling out of the hut at his command.

"Get lined up! A straight line, you miserable bunch of invalids!"

He shook his head in despair as the men shuffled about and tried to obey his command.

Privately, Sergeant-Major Bowler formed his own opinion of them. Not a bad intake, he thought.

These men had been civilians yesterday, and today they were soldiers, recruited to fight in the greatest war the world had known. And it was Sergeant-Major Bowler's job to knock them into shape.

The process would take several weeks and then they would be sorted out according to their respective skills and abilities—some would become clerks, some signallers, others despatch riders, others yet, the backbone of the Army — the footslogging infantrymen.

"Call out your names," Bowler roared at them.

He made a mental note of each name—a name he would remember up till the day they left him.

"Tufton!" called a voice and everyone laughed.

Bowler looked at the man who had called. He was small and weedy, with an anxious look on his face.

"So your name is Tufton," Bowler drawled. "Bert Tufton, no doubt, Britain's white hope of boxing?"

The rest of the squad roared with laughter again.

The little man went red.

"No. My name is Brian Tufton."

"And I'm Bert Tufton."

> **THE TUFTON "TWINS" SPELT DOUBLE TROUBLE FOR THE GERMANS!**

There was dead silence as everyone turned to look at the man at the end of the line who had spoken.

Built like the side of a barn, with a nose that had as much shape as a scrambled egg, this could only be the real Bert Tufton. Even Bowler looked at him with something approaching respect.

Tufton was one of the most aggressive and intelligent boxers Britain had ever produced and now here he was, just another raw recruit in a khaki uniform.

"Don't think your reputation cuts any ice with me!" Bowler bellowed. "You may be a dab hand in the ring, but on the drill square you're at my mercy—and there'll be no referee to look after you! Understood?"

Bert Tufton nodded.

"Yes, Sergeant-Major."

Bowler shook his head again.

"So I'm stuck with two Tuftons. Strikes me there's going to be an awful lot of confusion—unless you two play it safe. That means both of you will have to jump to it whenever I call your name. Understood?"

They understood. During the weeks that followed they did become efficient soldiers.

Bert Tufton was brilliant at everything he attempted—drill, marksmanship and, of course, he was superbly fit. The surprising thing was that the keenest trier in the whole squad was his namesake, Brian Tufton. It was as though Brian was trying to compensate for his lack of inches—he threw himself into everything they were taught with a furious energy.

Then came the day when they each had to fill in a card stating their civilian occupations. Bert wrote "Fighter"; Brian put down that he was engaged in scientific research into radio waves.

He could have remained a civilian with his specialist knowledge, but he had pulled every string he could to get into uniform. After years spent in laboratories, he longed for an active, open-air life, and he had jumped at this opportunity.

A few weeks later, the " Tufton Twins " were called to Bowler's office.

" I've got news for you two," he said. " Seems you're too important to finish off your basic training here. You've each been asked to volunteer for special postings to top-secret units. No one's even allowed to say what the units are. Do you want to volunteer ?"

" Yes, sar'nt-major !" they chorused.

Bowler shook his head as he completed the forms for their postings.

" Pity. Another couple of weeks and I could have made real soldiers out of you."

Bert Is Baffled

BERT got off the train at Little Bumpton with eagerness. Looking out of the station he could see that the village consisted of several cottages, and acres of green fields—nothing else.

This must be a really secret unit, he thought, being buried out in the wilds like this. It was probably made up of professional fighters like himself, men being trained to undertake some supremely dangerous task.

As he was preparing to walk down the road an ancient, khaki-coloured car came rattling up. It stopped beside Bert and the driver, a tubby, cigarette-smoking sergeant, popped his head out of the window.

" Are you Mister Tufton ?" he asked pleasantly.

" Yes, sarn't !" Bert snapped in reply, standing to attention.

The sergeant looked surprised as he opened the door.

" Hop in," he said. " You weren't thinking of walking to the camp, were you ?"

Bert was puzzled. He had never been spoken to by a sergeant in this way before, but he obediently climbed into the car.

" Shouldn't I walk it, sergeant ?" he asked.

" Good heavens no," the sergeant replied. " It's nearly a mile away —you'd tire yourself out ! By the way, my name is Culshaw, but everyone calls me Dodger. There's nobody in the British Army can beat me when it comes to dodging work !"

Bert didn't know what to say. He decided to keep quiet and see what happened.

The car rolled in through the gateway of a vast, rambling country house.

" This is the camp," Culshaw said, as he and Bert got out of the car by the imposing front door. " We call it a camp, but it's just this house with a few sheds at the back. We each have a room of our own."

Now Bert was sure he was dreaming. A room of his own in a country mansion—just what sort of unit had he come to ?

He followed Culshaw into the house. The door of a room opened and a middle-aged man came out. He wore spectacles and the uniform of a colonel.

Bert automatically came to attention and saluted. Then he noticed to his surprise that Culshaw had not reacted at all, and was still smoking his cigarette.

" This is Mister Tufton, sir," Culshaw said casually. " I've just brought him up from the station."

" Delighted to have you with us, Tufton," the colonel beamed, holding out his hand. It was a few seconds before Bert realised he was supposed to shake it.

" It is a dream—it has to be !" Bert thought, as the colonel took him by the arm and led him into another room.

" I hope you'll be happy here. You may as well meet the lads. I think most of them are here."

They were in a room where several men lounged around in armchairs. All were officers, and they were all dressed in a casual, almost careless, manner.

" Mister Tufton has just joined us," the colonel said. " I'm sure he'll be a valuable member of the team, and he'll find the work most interesting."

The officers all nodded in greeting to the bewildered Bert, and then the colonel noticed Bert's uniform.

" Tut, tut," he said. " I must see about your commission right away. It should come through within a couple of days."

" Commission ?" Bert gasped.

" Well, yes," the colonel said. " We all have commissions here, except the staff who actually run the house, of course. It's because of the work we do.

" After all, we're all highly skilled, and we'd hold positions of importance in civilian life. It's only right that we should have some importance in the Army and that's why we get a commission.

" Anyway, you'll want a rest after your journey. You'll be able to start work tomorrow."

" Er—would you mind telling me what sort of work, sir ?" Bert asked.

A phone started to ring in another room.

" You'll soon see," the colonel said. " It's the sort of thing you've been used to but I must go and answer that phone. I'll see you tomorrow and we'll have a little chat about things."

But the next day Bert didn't see the colonel. He was called to London for an important meeting, and Bert had to find his way round the house on his own. The other officers were friendly and treated him as an equal. After breakfast one of them, Captain Barnes, said to Bert, " Come along with us to the shop, and see what we're doing."

The shop turned out to be one of the long huts at the back of the house. As they went in, each of the officers donned a white coat. Inside were benches and tables, on which were pieces of what looked like radio equipment.

" Recognise what we're doing ?" Captain Barnes asked Bert.

" Well—something to do with radio—but I don't——"

" Very shrewd," Captain Barnes said. " It looks like radio—but you feel there's something odd about it. I thought you'd spot that. This is radar we're working on. You won't have heard of it in civvy street, but I can tell you it's winning the war for us."

He went off into a long technical description of the work that left Bert completely baffled.

" I'm sure you'll be able to contribute some really valuable work to this enterprise. Anyway

you just hang around and amuse yourself until the colonel gets back. He'll give you something definite to do," Barnes ended.

Bert wandered round the house for the rest of the day, and looked in at what the "domestic staff" were doing. These were the few people whose job seemed to be to look after the officers and run the general administration of the place.

Their attitude seemed to be the same as Sergeant Culshaw's, and judging from the quality of the breakfast he'd had that morning, Bert guessed that the cooks more than anybody took their job very easily.

But the main difference between the staff and the officers was that the staff recognised Bert.

"I've seen most of your fights," said "Scrounger" Wallis, a ferrety character who was supposed to keep the place tidy, but didn't. "I can see you as world champion yet. What made them post you here?"

"I dunno," Bert shrugged. "I still haven't worked out what sort of place this is."

"It's a research station, of course," said Culshaw. "The boffins—the officers you've met—are developing new types of radar. I don't know what that is except that it's top secret."

Commissioned

BERT walked away thoughtfully. Now he understood. Brian Tufton had been one of these boffin blokes before he'd joined the army, and this was just the sort of place he would belong to.

Someone at headquarters had got the two B. Tuftons mixed up and given them each other's posting.

Bert decided to tell the colonel and get the whole business sorted out.

But when the colonel got back he went straight into conference on some vitally important matter, and no one could get in to see him. Then after breakfast the next day Captain Barnes spoke to him.

"Your commission has come through. You're Lieutenant Tufton from now on. I'll let you have one of my old uniforms to wear until you get one of your own."

"Well—I don't think it's me that——"

Bert stopped.

"They've given me a commission, and I'm going to take it," Bert thought. He accepted the loan of the uniform, and that afternoon he went into the kitchen where Culshaw, Wallis and the rest of the staff were lounging about drinking tea.

"So you've got your uniform then," Wallis said. "I suppose we'll have to call you 'sir' now."

"Don't let it go to your head," Culshaw said. "This is a nice cushy number and no one wants to spoil it."

Bert looked round at them. He remembered the badly-prepared meals and he saw how untidy the place was.

"It's a cushy number for you lot," said Bert. "But it's not cushy for the boffins—because you aren't doing your jobs properly. I want to see a big improvement in conditions round here—and if I don't you lot will find yourselves in trouble! Understand?"

He said it in the same voice Bowler would have used, and it had the same effect. The staff jumped to their feet and started work right away.

The next day the place was spotless and the meals first class.

That afternoon Bert was summoned to the shop where the colonel was waiting for him.

"Thought we'd sort something out for you to start work on, Tufton," the colonel said genially. "You're familiar with the cathode ray tube, of course?"

Bert thought he was dreaming when he arrived at his new camp— a country mansion.

Bert shook his head.

"The only tube I'm familiar with, sir, is the one I get my toothpaste from."

The officers looked at each other, then the colonel said, "Er—what university were you at, Tufton?"

Bert laughed.

"I've never been near one in my life, sir. I left Canal Street School, Bloxwell, when I was fourteen and then I became a boxer."

"A boxer?" The colonel coughed politely. "Very interesting. Well, you pop along now and take a walk round the grounds. I'll—er—see you later."

When Bert had gone the colonel shrugged.

"Someone in Whitehall has mixed up the papers again," he said. "Pity he'll have to go—he's a very pleasant chap."

"Does he have to go, sir?" asked Captain Barnes. "He's doing a first-class job of organising the staff. He'll have the place running like clockwork soon and that will give us far more time to concentrate on our work."

"That's true," the colonel said. "I noticed a vast improvement in the meals. Yes, I think we'll keep Tufton here now that he's been given to us. It doesn't do to look a gift horse in the mouth."

This was where his small stature gave him an advantage over the brawny soldiers who made up the rest of the Commando. He could get through places that were impassable to a bigger man.

Brian dropped into the shell-hole in front of him as the bullets seemed to sweep even lower above his head.

In the shellhole waiting was one of the instructors who was playing the part of an enemy soldier. The instructor dived at him, but Brian swayed to one side, at the same time grabbing one of his assailant's outstretched arms. With a quick twist Brian sent the instructor sprawling on his back, then he was

should all go home and leave the war to him."

Brian was exhausted but happy. This was the sort of physical challenge that he had looked forward to when he joined up.

When he had first arrived at the Commando school there had been the hoots of laughter and disbelieving looks that he had expected. What was a tiddler like him doing among the big fish, was the question that was asked.

There must have been a mistake, was the general opinion of the instructors, but while various people were trying to find out what had

Brian's small stature had made him seem the most unlikely commando, but he soon showed how tough he could be.

Commando Course

BRIAN TUFTON crawled along the muddy ground as bullets whistled over his head. Alongside him were the other members of No. 406 Commando.

They had to get to the other end of the assault course within ten minutes or they would have Sergeant Blake to reckon with and, compared to him, Sergeant-Major Bowler was like Florence Nightingale.

Facing them was a tangled barbed-wire fence. Brian reached it first and started to wriggle his way underneath. Soon he was ahead of everyone else.

out of the shellhole and continuing on his way.

He came to a deep gully next, with only a single rope crossing it. Brian did not hesitate. He swung on to it and started to haul himself across hand over hand.

At last he reached the other bank and without pause raced on.

A group of instructors advanced on him like a rugby pack out of the gathering gloom of the late afternoon. Brian went straight into the middle of them and emerged on the other side while they were still vainly trying to get hold of him.

Then he was over the finishing line.

"Tufton is first again," Sergeant Blake said drily. "I reckon we

happened, Brian was allowed to start the course.

Within a couple of days the word was quietly passed around to drop the inquiries. Maybe Brian shouldn't have been sent there in the first place, but now that he was the Commandos wanted to keep him. His remarkable determination and tenacity marked him out from the start in everything he tackled.

At last the hard weeks of training were completed and No. 406 Commando was ready and keen for action. But no action came. For months they stayed in camp keeping themselves at peak combat fitness, but it began to look as if they would never get a chance to match their strength against the Germans. Then one day, when least expected, they were briefed for a special operation.

Into Action

THE Royal Navy destroyer swung round in an arc and gradually came to a stop. It was night, and about half a mile away the darker outline of the French coast could be seen.

"Landing party stand by," said a naval lieutenant, as the crew lowered nets over the side.

There were several slight splashes as rubber boats were dropped, and within seconds the Commandos were swarming down the nets into them. As each boat was filled it was pushed silently away from the ship and the men began to paddle towards the shore.

Brian was in the first boat.

As soon as they hit the beach they dragged the boat clear of the water and waited for the rest of the Commandos to join them.

"All clear, sir," said Sergeant Blake, who had been in the first boat and who had crept up to the rocks at the top of the beach and cautiously surveyed the land.

Major Purvis, the Commando leader, aimed his torch at the destroyer and flashed a brief signal. Immediately another boat was lowered. Six men got in and headed for the beach.

"Hurry along, you boffins," Major Purvis said as the boat finally grounded and the six men came ashore.

Among the boffins was Bert.

When the colonel had discussed with his officers just who would go on the operation from the laboratory, Bert had been the first to volunteer. The colonel had been doubtful, pointing out that this was a specialist's job, but the others had supported Bert. As well as having acquired a certain amount of technical knowledge, his physical strength might come in very useful.

When everybody was assembled on the beach, Major Purvis addressed them.

"We Commandos will do all the fighting that is necessary. You boffins will go straight in when we've cleared the way and collect what you want. Then it's straight back to the beach."

To his Commandos he added, "Remember—our job is to get every last one of these boffins back safely, even at the expense of our own lives. We can't afford to let any of them fall into German hands, because they know too much.

"Right—let's go!"

They made their way through the sand dunes, over the rocks and then across the empty fields.

Fifteen minutes later Major Purvis held up his hand to signal them to halt.

"The radar station is dead ahead now," he said quietly. "We'll go straight in the main gate."

The German sentry at the gate started at the slight noise behind him. Before he could even turn around, an arm went round his throat. The arm pulled tighter and tighter until the German blacked out and collapsed in a heap.

Major Purvis led his men quickly through the gate.

"That's what we're aiming for —the square building over there next to the masts," he whispered and led his men towards it.

A German soldier came out of a hut and stopped dead.

"Achtung!" he called. A burst of fire killed him. Sergeant Blake swung his smoking tommy-gun round as a group of German soldiers tumbled out of the hut opposite. Before they fully realised what was happening he had raked them with fire.

By now the station was coming to life. The Commandos broke up swiftly into several detachments as planned, and tackled each group of Germans as they appeared. Soon bitter hand-to-hand fighting was going on all round as the group of boffins, with a detachment of Commandos, reached the small building where the radar equipment was installed. It was a solid brick building with a locked door.

Brian carefully pointed his gun at the lock and pulled the trigger. The lock shattered and they hauled the door open and poured inside. Within seconds the boffins were busily dismantling the equipment and putting small parts of it into canvas bags, while others carefully weighed up the technicalities of the system.

By now the Commandos outside had overcome the German defenders and Major Purvis looked

The Commandos meant to go in the main gate and no German sentry was going to stop them!

"I will have you shot."

Brian refused to answer the German's questions on radar — and the German refused to believe he wasn't a scientist.

in to see how the boffins were doing.

"Five more minutes and we must go," he said.

Suddenly there came a burst of gunfire from the other side of the camp.

"Strange, I thought we'd cleared them all out of there," he said as he rushed out.

"More Jerries, sir," Sergeant Blake reported, pointing to the wire fence. Coming towards them across the field was a vast mass of German soldiers.

"Just our luck," said Major Purvis. "There must be a German infantry camp nearby. They weren't mentioned on the reconnaissance reports which means they must have only just moved in.

"Right! Tell the boffins to pack up and move out. They should have enough stuff by now anyway."

Captain Barnes, the leader of the boffins, nodded when Sergeant Blake brought him the word.

"We've got a pretty good idea now of how far Jerry has got with his radar," he said.

As the boffins moved out, Brian and two other Commandos placed explosive charges in the radar

building and at the base of the masts.

As the whole party started to withdraw there was a series of shattering explosions. Down crashed the masts and the radar building erupted in a hail of bricks and dust.

A flying piece of brick hit one of the Commandos and knocked him out.

"Keep moving," Major Purvis roared to the boffins, as his men ushered them out of the camp. In the darkness he didn't see Bert break away and rush back to the Commando who had been hit by the brick.

"Come on, mate," Bert said, hauling him to his feet. The man, just coming to, was rocking on his feet. Bert slung him over his shoulder and started to run after the others, but at that moment a mortar bomb crashed alongside him. The blast sent him staggering and he tripped flat on his face.

Brian glanced back and saw that Bert, one of the boffins, was being left behind. Major Purvis's orders had been quite clear — the Commandos had to make sure the boffins got away, even if it cost them their own lives.

Brian raced towards him, firing his tommy-gun at the advancing Germans. Then another mortar bomb burst and for Brian everything dissolved into blackness.

Mistaken Identity

BRIAN swayed as he stood before the desk of Colonel Brandt, the commandant of the radar station.

"Stand still, Britisher!" Brandt roared. "You will answer my questions or I will have you shot like the spy you are!"

Brian wearily shook his head once again.

"I've told you, I know nothing about radar——"

He went crashing against the wall as one of the guards alongside him hit him with the butt of his rifle.

"Liar!" snarled Brandt. "You must be one of the scientists the British brought on their raid to steal our secrets!"

As the guard hauled him in front of the commandant's desk again, Brian protested.

"I'm no scientist—I'm a Commando, a fighting man!"

Brandt's face went red with fury.

"I will not be made a fool of!" he bellowed. "Take him back to his cell again!"

As the German guards dragged him back to his cell, Brian glanced round the radar station. The Commandos had done their job well, judging from the smoking heap of rubble that had been the main radar building. Now men were trying to sort out the wreckage and Brian recognised Bert among them. The Germans were making him do the toughest work of moving the broken concrete beams.

As he reached the cell, Brian knew what would happen. The two guards sent him reeling with their rifle butts. After pounding him into semi-consciousness, they stepped out, and the cell door clanged shut. There they left him to consider the folly of refusing to talk.

A couple of hours later Brian heard the cell next to his being opened, and the sound of someone being thrust inside. After the sound of the guard's boots had died away, Brian called out, "Is that you, Bert?"

"Yes. The fools think I'm the Commando," Bert answered. "They're making me work on clearing up the wreckage. They must think I don't know anything about radar, but I picked up a fair bit at Little Bumpton."

"I reckon it's about time we thought of escaping. Any ideas?" Brian asked.

"I'm in no hurry," Bert said. "In that wrecked building there are some drawings our lads would like to take a look at. I'm hoping to get hold of them tomorrow—I think I know where they're kept."

The next day Brian was dragged once more to the commandant's office. Once again the questioning started, but all the Germans could get out of Brian was his name, rank and number.

As Brandt was about to explode once more, an n.c.o. brought in a signal and laid it on his desk. Brandt read it and scowled.

"Right, Britisher," he snarled. "You wouldn't give any information to me, but now you are to be handed over to the experts. This signal instructs me to send you immediately to the Gestapo headquarters in Berlin. They will do things that will make you glad to talk!"

He turned to the n.c.o.

"They want the other prisoner, too—the Commando officer. I've no doubt they have something special in store for him. Get him from where he is working, and have the two of them taken to the airfield. An aircraft is waiting to take them to Berlin."

Brian was hustled out into the back of a lorry. A minute later Bert was dragged in to join him. Half a dozen armed guards got in with them.

"I got the papers," Bert whispered as they bumped together during the journey.

The aircraft they were hustled into was a Junkers three-engined transport. Once inside, the two prisoners were placed at opposite ends of the cabin, with the guards between them.

Bert was the one they watched closely. He was the Commando, the man trained to fight, the Germans reckoned. To make sure he stayed under control, they snapped a pair of handcuffs on his wrists.

Bert protested strongly as the aircraft took off.

"I'm no criminal!" he bellowed. "What are you chaining me up for?"

As he started to struggle, the guards thrust him back into his seat with their gun barrels.

Brian sat peacefully near the front, a mild, insignificant-looking man. His mind was working quickly. He could see Bert was deliberately making a fuss to occupy the guards' attention as much as possible. This left the initiative with Brian—and he would have to do something quickly. It would not take very long to reach Berlin.

The Tables Are Turned

THE guard facing Brian stood up to stretch himself, his carbine cradled under his arm. As he did so, Brian's feet shot out and his boots hit the German's shins with a great crack.

The guard staggered forward with a cry of pain. In a split second Brian had grabbed his left arm and swung the German round. He brought his other hand up and hit the German's right shoulder with the side of it. The carbine fell from the guard's numbed hand.

Brian kicked the German away from him as he snatched up the carbine. He stood up to face the group at the rear of the aircraft, who had only just started to grasp what was happening.

One of them rushed forward. Brian stood his ground until the German was almost upon him, when he dropped down and lunged forward. The guard went flying over Brian's head to crash on to his previous victim.

A shot whistled over Brian's head as he hurled himself low at the guards around Bert. As he reached them Bert stood up suddenly and brought his manacled fists crashing down on to the back of the neck of the one who was about to fire again. Using the gun as a club, Brian hammered another one to the floor.

As the two guards at the front rushed back Brian dipped into the pocket of the guard on the floor and snatched out the key which he threw to Bert.

"Get yourself free!" he snapped as he turned to face the next onslaught.

The two guards and Brian

A gun in his back was all the argument the German pilot needed to make him change course.

collapsed in a struggling heap, but by then Bert had his hands free. He picked up the guards, one at a time, and clipped straight lefts to their jaws.

As Brian picked himself up, he saw they had complete control of the cabin.

" Get in that corner," he ordered the guards who were not unconscious, pointing the carbine at them. Sullenly the Germans obeyed.

Bert picked up one of the guns and Brian said, "Keep them covered."

Then he made his way forward to the flight deck. As he reached it, the communicating door swung open and the wireless operator brought up his drawn pistol.

The crew members had heard the noise and guessed there was trouble. But before the German could pull the trigger, Brian grabbed his wrist and twisted it up his back.

" Get back in there !" he ordered.

He stepped into the forward cabin after the wireless operator and pressed the muzzle of the carbine against the back of the pilot's head.

" Change course for Britain," Brian said in a voice that was cold and merciless. "And don't try to do anything clever. There are two parachutes in here and my mate and I will use them after we've shot you lot—and we will if you don't do exactly as you're told."

The pilot didn't need telling twice. He swung the aircraft round and headed for the Channel.

Shot Down

THE German fighters caught up with them halfway across the Channel. Three

Focke-Wulfs swung down on them out of the clouds and started to circle the Junkers.

" The wireless operator must have got a message off just as the rumpus started," Brian said, as he and Bert watched the fighters through the window.

" They are signalling to us to turn round," the Junkers pilot said.

" Ignore them," Brian ordered. " Your destination is the white cliffs of Dover."

When they saw the Junkers carrying on, the fighters began their attack. One by one they swooped down on the transport, their guns blazing.

" We do not stand a chance," the Junkers pilot said, as his windscreen shattered into fragments.

The Focke-Wulfs lined up for another attack, then suddenly started to climb away from the transport.

" The R.A.F. has arrived," Brian said, pointing to a squadron of Spitfires which was dropping on them through a gap in the clouds. The two groups of fighters met head-on, and the sky was filled with a screaming tangle of planes and bullets.

Within two minutes, one of the Focke-Wulfs exploded, another was smoking badly as it spiralled towards the sea, and the third turned tail for the French coast.

" There's Blighty straight ahead !" said Bert. "It looks as though we've made it !"

" Don't be too sure," Brian said. He pointed to the Spitfires which were now turning their attention to the Junkers. "We're wearing the swastika, too !"

But the British pilots didn't fire right away. They were obviously puzzled as to why a German transport should be headed for

Britain, under fire from its own fighters.

Bert and Brian thought desperately of some way they could signal the R.A.F. pilots, but there was none. The Spitfire pilots finally decided not to take any chances, and began their attack.

The first burst of fire hit the Junkers' port engine, and it burst into flames.

" Ditch it !" Brian ordered the German pilot. " If they see we're coming down they might stop firing."

" I can see a beach ahead of us," Bert said. "With a bit of luck we might make it that far."

The British pilots held their fire as they saw the Junkers losing height. It was skimming the waves as the beach drew near. The German pilot pushed his control column forward and the aircraft bit into the water, throwing up a tremendous wave. As it jerked to a halt, Bert swung the door open and jumped into the sea.

" It's a lovely day for a paddle !" he said with a grin to Brian. The water came just up to his knees.

* * * * *

When Bert and Brian got back to their units, there was news for each of them. The mistakes in their original postings had been discovered, and they were ordered to each other's unit.

Brian arrived at Little Bumpton just as Bert was leaving.

" Well," he said, "it'll make a change for me to get back to research again."

Bert grinned.

" I've enjoyed myself here, but I could do with a bit more action. And if the Commandos can do for me what they did for you, Brian, I reckon I'll be finding it !"

THE TRAIL OF MAD MALONE

A game of cards was being played in a store by the banks of the River Lualava, in Central Africa. Dupont, the French owner of the store, and Raus, a German who ran a nearby farm, made up one pair. Their opponents were Rattigan, an American, and Lord Harry Selby, an Englishman who was Rattigan's partner in an almost worked-out copper mine. Their game received an unexpected interruption . . .

WHERE IS THE STRIKE, THAT'S THE POINT? WE WOULD ALL BE RICH MEN IF WE COULD ONLY FIND IT.

WE COULD NEVER BACK-TRACK THE TRAIL OF MAD MALONE OURSELVES. I KNOW OF ONLY ONE PERSON WHO COULD—SHIWA SANDS!

Shiwa Sands was the son of the late Saul Sands, a famous tracker and white hunter. He was only fifteen, but had already built up quite a reputation in the same field. Dupont sent one of his native employees to Shiwa's camp and soon the boy hunter appeared with Tipu, a Kalahari bushman who followed him everywhere.

I BELIEVE YOU HAVE A JOB FOR ME, MISTER DUPONT?

INDEED I HAVE, MISTER SANDS. A JOB FOR WHICH YOU CAN NAME YOUR OWN PRICE.

I'M NOT INTERESTED. WHEN I CAN NAME MY OWN PRICE IT ALWAYS MEANS SOMETHING CRUEL OR CROOKED, SUCH AS GAME SLAUGHTER OR IVORY SMUGGLING, IS INVOLVED.

BUT I ASSURE YOU, MISTER SANDS, THE JOB IS HONEST.

THAT'S WHAT THEY ALL SAY.

Shiwa was told how Mad Malone had arrived at the store and how the four men had formed the plan to back-track his trail to the diamond deposit. After much thought Shiwa came to a decision.

I SHALL GO WITH THE BWANAS, TIPU. YOU MUST WAIT HERE UNTIL I RETURN. YOUR PRESENCE WILL NOT BE REQUIRED ON THE JOURNEY.

NO, BOSS. I COME—YOU NEED ME.

I SHALL BE VERY ANGRY IF YOU ATTEMPT TO COME, TIPU. YOU MUST STAY HERE.

ALL RIGHT, BOSS.

FUNNY LITTLE GUY, AIN'T HE? HE'S TRAVELLED A LONG WAY FROM THE KALAHARI DESERT.

PEOPLE OFTEN TRAVEL, AND FOR MANY STRANGE REASONS. SOMETIMES THEY EVEN TRAVEL FROM AMERICA TO AFRICA, MISTER RATTIGAN!

"I'm going after the diamonds."

Shiwa realised he had no alternative, so they began the climb up the cliff face . . .

I FOLLOW YOU. BOSS. I DISOBEY YOU. YOU ANGRY WITH ME?

NOT THIS TIME, TIPU! NOT THIS TIME.

I CAN FEEL THE POISON WORKING IN ME. I SEEM TO BE GOING ALL NUMB. I RECKON I'VE HAD IT.

THEY ARE MURDEROUS SCOUNDRELS, MISTER SANDS, BUT SURELY WE CANNOT JUST LET THEM DIE!

ONLY THEIR IMAGINATION WILL KILL THEM, MISTER RAUS. THE ARROWS TIPU SHOT AT THEM WERE HARMLESS. HE ONLY USES POISON WHEN I PERMIT IT.

YOU TRICKED US, YOU LITTLE WRETCH. IF I GET MY HANDS ON YOU...

YES, YOU WERE TRICKED JUST AS YOU TRIED TO TRICK US. THE ONLY DIFFERENCE BEING THAT YOUR TRICK FAILED. YOU'RE NOT LIKELY TO GET YOUR HANDS ON ME WHILE I HOLD THIS RIFLE ON YOU.

WHAT DO YOU WANT ME TO DO WITH THIS PAIR NOW?

YOU COULD TURN THEM OVER TO THE POLICE I SUPPOSE BUT WHY BOTHER? NO ONE HAS BEEN HARMED EXCEPT THEMSELVES. COULD YOU RUN THEM OVER THE BORDER, SHIWA? I DON'T THINK THEY'LL EVER HAVE THE NERVE TO COME BACK TO THIS PART OF THE COUNTRY.

I WILL DO THAT WITH NO TROUBLE AT ALL. NOW YOU SHALL BE VERY RICH INSTEAD OF THIS PAIR.

THIS IS TRUE, BUT I AM ALSO RATHER SAD.

WHERE ARE WE LIKELY TO FIND ANOTHER TWO WHO CAN PLAY CARDS AS WELL AS THOSE RASCALS?

The Man In The Mine

In 1944, during the Second World War, the Royal Navy had a secret weapon. It looked like an ordinary sea mine, but it was actually a kind of one-man submarine. Captain Tom Nielson, of the Royal Marine Commandos, was the man in the mine. One of his missions took him to the Far East, where the Allies were beginning to hit back at the Japanese. The plan was to fly him and his mine into the operational area to locate an R.A.F. plane that had been shot down.

WE DO REGULAR RUNS ALONG THE JAP-HELD COAST, PLANTING MINES. WE'RE GOING TO DROP YOU ALONG WITH THE REST, AND HOPE THEY WON'T SMELL A RAT. WE'VE RIGGED A PARACHUTE, BUT THERE'S NO TIME FOR TESTS. YOU'VE TO GET IN THERE FAST, NIELSON.

I UNDERSTAND, SIR.

Just before dusk, the aircraft took off.

WE'LL DROP YOU HERE, ABOUT WHERE THE JAPS SHOT OUR PLANE DOWN. THE PLANE WAS CARRYING GENERAL TURNBULL FROM ALLIED HEAD-QUARTERS, AND HE HAD WITH HIM PLANS FOR OUR NEXT OFFENSIVE. IF THE JAPS SALVAGE THE PLANE AND FIND THOSE PLANS OUR WHOLE STRATEGY IS IN PERIL.

WELL, I'LL HAVE TO GET THERE FIRST!

HEAVY FLAK! THE JAPS HAVE BROUGHT UP NEW ANTI-AIRCRAFT BATTERIES.

WE'VE BEEN HIT! GET ABOARD YOUR MINE. WE'RE NEARLY AT THE DROPPING ZONE.

Nielson submerged quickly.

50

"The crew didn't have a chance."

I HEARD THE BOAT GO AWAY. I'LL RELEASE THE PARACHUTES AND SURFACE.

ALL QUIET. AND IT'S NEARLY DAYLIGHT. I'LL ANCHOR HERE AND START MY SEARCH FOR THE DITCHED AIRCRAFT.

THE MINE SHOULD HIDE ME FROM ANYBODY ASHORE.

I'LL QUARTER THE SEA BED IN A METHODICAL SEARCH.

After some time—

THERE IT IS!

THE PILOT AND THE NAVIGATOR ARE STILL AT THEIR POSTS. THE CREW DIDN'T HAVE A CHANCE.

HERE ARE GENERAL TURNBULL'S DOCUMENTS. THE JAPS HAVEN'T GOT HERE YET. PROBABLY NO DIVERS AVAILABLE. BUT THERE'S NO SIGN OF TURNBULL'S BODY.

51

THE AIRCRAFT IS SHIFTING! HECK, THERE'S A CABLE OUTSIDE! A GRAPNEL HAS HOOKED THE PLANE!

THE JAPS HAVE BROUGHT ALONG A SALVAGE VESSEL. THEY'RE WINCHING THE AIRCRAFT UP. I'VE GOT TO GET OUT OF HERE BEFORE THEY FISH ME TO THE SURFACE!

THE CABLE OUTSIDE IS HOLDING THE HATCH SHUT!

THE PILOT'S WINDSCREEN IS ALREADY DAMAGED BY BULLET HOLES. I'LL ENLARGE THE HOLE.

I'M THROUGH!

JUST IN TIME!

THEY'RE TAKING THE AIRCRAFT AWAY FOR INSPECTION. I CAN GET BACK IN THE MINE AS SOON AS THEY'VE CLEARED OFF.

YES, THESE ARE GENERAL TURNBULL'S PAPERS BUT WHAT ABOUT THE GENERAL HIMSELF? HIS BODY COULD HAVE BEEN THROWN CLEAR. BUT I DIDN'T SEE IT WHILE I WAS SEARCHING. SUPPOSE HE SURVIVED? IF THE JAPJ GOT HIM, THAT'S ALMOST AS DANGEROUS AS IF THEY HAD THESE PAPERS. I'VE GOT TO MAKE SURE.

Nielson waited until dark.

THE ONLY WAY TO DISCOVER IF GENERAL TURNBULL IS HELD PRISONER IS TO GO ASHORE.

THE JAPS ARE BOUND TO HAVE SENTRIES OUT. I'LL HAVE TO GO CAREFULLY.

WHAT'S THAT RUSTLING NOISE? HECK, AN ARMY OF LAND CRABS COMING OUT OF THEIR BURROWS FOR ONE OF THEIR NIGHTLY RAIDS ON THE COCONUT GROVES!

UGH! I'LL HAVE TO LIE STILL AND LET THEM CRAWL OVER ME! I CAN'T RISK GIVING MY POSITION AWAY TO THE JAPS.

PHEW! GOOD JOB THEY DON'T FANCY HUMAN FLESH! HALLO, THEY'VE REACHED ONE OF THE SENTRY POSTS!

AIEEE!

THE CRABS HAVE DONE ME A GOOD TURN. THEY'VE SHOWN ME THE SENTRY'S POSITION. AND HE'S RETREATING. HE LIKES THEM EVEN LESS THAN I DO!

"They've been torturing him."

The one-man rescue mission.

WE HATE WHISTLING WILLIE!

THE MAN THE CROWD LOVES TO HATE!

'M Bill Yeadon, and I'm a Rugby League referee. And if you think soccer refs come in for barracking, then you've never seen a real, full-blooded game of Rugby League.

You see, the trouble with many fans of this rough, tough sport is that they take it so seriously. They know a lot about the game, too, and the referee who misses a knock-on or a forward pass soon gets the "bird" from them.

Take it from me, there isn't a more exciting game in existence than Rugby League football. There's something about the sight of that oval ball flashing from man to man that makes your blood tingle.

That's why the fans get so hot under the collar when the whistle goes too often. And it's always the referee who gets the blame for stopping the game—not the blokes who cause the infringements.

It takes a good bit of courage to whistle up a home player in full flight for the line with the opposing defence scattered behind him. The partisans in the crowd probably haven't noticed the forward pass which gave him the ball.

And just try hauling a hefty, sixteen-stone front-row forward out of a scrummage and talking to him like a Dutch uncle, when you're only half his size!

The match which lives in my memory for stark, strong-arm, robust rugby is the clash between Denton Rovers and Westford Town which took place a few seasons ago in the third round of the Challenge Cup.

Sometimes I wake up sweating when I dream of those hair-raising crowd scenes. You see, I was in the middle at that match. In more ways than one!

Now Denton Rovers have never been a fashionable club. Their average home gate rarely exceeds eight thousand, so they haven't a great deal of money to splash around on the transfer market.

Most of the club's players are home-grown, recruited from the collieries and steelworks which ring the grimy little town. Their style of play is right in character with their surroundings — rough, rugged, and uncompromising.

The narrow, bumpy, Denton ground has proved the graveyard of the Wembley ambitions of many visiting clubs. That partisan crowd of hard-bitten miners and steel workers is worth at least ten points start to the home side.

As a complete contrast, Westford Town are one of the all-time "greats" of the Rugby League game. They have a fine tradition for playing fast, open rugby, and have won every honour in the game several times over.

This particular season I have in mind, they had one of the best sides in their history as a club. Under the dynamic leadership of their captain and stand-off half, Jack Langan, who is still one of the finest players ever to wear a number six on his jersey, they were well set at the head of the league table.

Including their skipper, they had five current international stars in the side, and had already won their first and second round ties by cricket scores. As a cup bet, they were favourites at five to two.

All the same, they had come unstuck quite a few times on the Denton ground where the conditions —and the home fans—were against their open style of play.

Well, when I was allotted this third-round tie between Denton and Westford I wasn't too happy about it. I knew the Denton crowd pretty well—come to that, they knew me, too.

On the Denton ground I rejoiced in the nickname of "Whistling Willie," no doubt due to the

He had asked for it, of course, by flattening the opposing full-back with one blow of his mighty fist. You can hand-off an opponent in Rugby League, but we draw the line at punching. So I gave him his marching orders. And the Denton crowd didn't like it.

Capacity Crowd

THE day of the match was a real stinker, an omen for the game to come. Denton was at its drab worst, with grey skies that looked full of rain and a pall of smoke hanging over the town.

Heavy pre-match rain had soaked the pitch and when twenty-six pairs of studded boots got to work on

The ground was jammed to capacity with about twenty thousand spectators. The black and white colours of Denton predominated, but there was a good sprinkling of the Westford blue.

About five thousand fans had made the journey with the league leaders, but the other fifteen thousand were solidly behind the Rovers. The long low stand on the east side of the ground was a mass of black and white favours.

This was the traditional home of the Denton "Old Guard," the eight thousand or so fanatics who urged their team to win at all costs.

When the fourteen-stone Plug Palmer led his side out in their black jerseys and white shorts, the ground erupted with enthusiasm. They were a burly lot, even for a Rugby League side. The six for-

A reception for Whistling Willie!

frequency with which I had to step in and quell their rampaging heavyweights when they were getting out of hand.

During the course of my last visit to Denton I had incurred the displeasure of the home fans by sending off their skipper and loose-forward, Plug Palmer, a tearaway character who looked as though he was carved out of solid teak.

it, the playing area would probably trample into a quagmire. It was the sort of weather that the Denton dreadnoughts revelled in.

An air of feverish excitement hung over the ground. The third round of the Challenge Cup is the one immediately preceding the semi-finals, so there is a great deal at stake. It's only two steps from Wembley.

wards in their pack tipped the scales at a combined weight of ninety stone! Their backs weren't midgets, either.

The greeting reserved for Jack Langan and the Westford team as they trotted out in their blue and white hooped jerseys and white pants was somewhat restrained, although the Westford fans made plenty of noise.

"If Denton lose today, I hope there's a helicopter for us!"

The Denton players couldn't get the ball — but they aimed to get the Westford player instead!

There were some heavy-weights in the Westford side, too, but taking it all round they were much the lighter team. And a great deal faster—although the heavy going would slow them down quite a bit. They looked fit and confident.

A few jeering cries sprang up from the home fans, but these soon died away when I appeared out of the tunnel.

What a reception! As a referee, I'm used to getting the bird, but this time the Denton supporters really surpassed themselves. A torrent of boos, cat-calls and whistles assailed my eardrums, and I received a couple of broadsides of orange peel for good measure as I made my way to the middle. To the hottest spot of my life!

The other officials were touch-judges Dave Christie and Les Reid. Both were experienced men, but even they were taken aback by the reception accorded to "Whistling Willie."

"Crikey!" exclaimed Dave Christie, as he walked across with me to take the line at the "safer" side of the ground. "If Denton lose today, I hope there's a helicopter waiting for us!"

I called the two captains to the middle, and the home skipper, Plug Palmer, spun the coin in a ham-like hand. He towered over the stocky Jack Langan, who called correctly and decided to play with what little breeze there was.

Frayed Tempers

POCKETING the coin, I waited for the two teams to line up and checked my watch. In Rugby League you play forty minutes each way because it's far more strenuous than soccer.

Here's the line-up of the two teams that day—I can remember

every player who took part without looking up the book. As opposed to the more widely known Rugby Union game, there are only thirteen players on each side, and the numbering starts with the full-back right down to the loose-forward who wears the number thirteen jersey.

Denton Rovers—Naggs; Black, Boyce, Peddle, Dick; Raine, Scotney; Blunden, Peake, Casey, Took, Dixon, and Palmer (capt.).

Westford Town—Lacey; Topping, Donavan, Cask, Draxford; Langan (capt.), Jowsey; Flanagan, Roberts, Carter, Gunn, Pacey, and Hobbs.

I blew the whistle and to a tremendous roar, Scotney, the chunky Denton scrum-half, kicked off.

In a surging black tide the Denton dreadnoughts steamed up the field and engulfed Geoff Pacey, who fielded the kick. The Westford second-row man dis-

The try that wasn't!

appeared beneath the combined weight of three of the Rovers' heavy-weight forwards.

Under the laws of Rugby League you are allowed to retain the ball after a tackle instead of letting it go loose. When you regain your feet, you "play the ball," that is, drop it on to the ground directly in front of you and heel it behind you to one of your own side acting as a "dummy half."

You can play it forward, too, if you choose, but this is usually reserved for a surprise move near the opposing line. I've seen quite

the Rovers. I should have come down equally hard on the Westford side if I had caught them.

Lacey, the strong-kicking Westford full-back, came up to take the resultant free-kick. Howls of rage from the Denton fans greeted the decision.

The uncomplimentary remarks grew even louder when Lacey found touch five yards from the Denton line with a raking kick. The two sets of forwards packed down for the first scrummage of the game. Scotney, as the defending scrum-half, prepared to put the ball in.

line without a finger being laid upon him. Lacey added insult to injury by tacking on the goal points from directly under the sticks. Westford were five points up !

The Denton fans bellowed their disapproval. And, judging by their remarks, they were blaming the poor old ref instead of the gap that yawned in the Rovers' defence !

To give the Denton players credit, they didn't let this surprise score take the steam out of them. They buckled to with a will and belted into the attack straight from the restart.

The Denton players were sure it was a try — but they were in for a shock!

a few tries stolen in this way by the man playing the ball.

Straight away I had a job keeping the eager Denton forwards onside. Each team has to stand at least three yards behind the men involved in play-the-ball to give the game room to develop.

After waving back Plug Palmer and his tearaways, I motioned for the ball to be played—and promptly surprised the Denton team by whipping round smartly and catching nearly half a dozen of them offside !

Let me make this clear, I wasn't after making things hot solely for

It's worth remembering that, under league rules, the ball can only pass straight into touch in the case of free kicks. In all other cases the ball must bounce before crossing the line. If it doesn't, then the ref whistles for "ball-back" which means that a scrum takes place from where the kick was taken.

Roberts, the Westford international hooker, won the first strike, and little Jowsey promptly whipped the ball out of the scrum and shot across the field at a tangent.

Drawing the defence, he shot a brilliant reverse pass to Jack Langan, who was over the Denton

For quite a time Denton pressed, making hard yet unspectacular progress and egged on by their fervent fans. Twice, the Westford trainer was called on to attend to his players who had been in head-on collision with the Denton dreadnoughts. Westford just couldn't get a look at the ball.

Suddenly the ball was whipped across to a burly, muddy figure who took the pass on the burst and scattered three Westford defenders before grounding the ball over the line.

It was Plug Palmer, and the Denton crowd shrieked with

Denton get a try!

Jack Langan passed the ball towards his winger — but would it get there?

ecstasy as his team-mates patted him on the back. But the cheering died away when they saw me motioning for a scrummage five yards out from the line.

The pass that had sent Plug Palmer over had been definitely forward. Palmer had known it, too, but he'd been hoping to get away with it! But it didn't stop the home crowd from howling for my blood!

Plug Palmer and his men milled round me playing up the incident for all they were worth. Some of the Denton side probably thought the try had been a good one. I was

too old a hand to argue the point with them, though, and whistled for them to get on with the scrummage.

From the scrum the ball came out on the Westford side, and, quick as a flash, the ball was slipped to Lacey who put in a towering kick which found touch on the halfway line.

Another scrum which Roberts again won, and Westford clicked into gear with a brilliant crossfield passing movement which ended with Naggs, the Denton full-back crash-tackling left-winger Draxford into touch a yard out.

This time I detected the Westford loose-forward, Hobbs, lurking in an off-side position round the scrum and awarded a penalty kick to Denton. I was awarded with a burst of sarcastic cheering from the home crowd.

Plug Palmer took the kick and relieved the pressure on his line with a thirty-yard touch-finder. Then followed a typical spell of Denton pressure which had the league leaders defending grimly.

With the crowd hooting like dervishes, feeling started to creep into the game. The Rovers were fully aware that they couldn't match Westford for skill, and closed the game right up.

How they expected to score themselves using these tactics, I didn't know, but they kept right on playing on top of the classier outfit.

Westford tempers started to get frayed, too, and I was kept pretty busy living up to the name of Whistling Willie. Both sides incurred my displeasure as the mudbath continued.

Just before half-time Denton scored a gift try. From inside his own half, Jack Langan attempted to open the game out and free his team from the Denton stranglehold.

He flung out a high, lofted pass to Topping on the right wing, and, quick as a flash, John Dick, on the Denton left flank, had intercepted the ball and bolted over the Westford line.

With a magnificent kick from the touchline, Plug Palmer sent the muddy ball soaring over the crossbar and smack between the uprights to equalise the scores.

Some of the home fans were so enthusiastic that they ran on to the field. The police had to clear them off before the two teams could get

The Story Of The Cover

SPECIAL AIR SERVICE

TOWARDS the end of 1941, Lieutenant David Stirling was given permission to form a special unit of his own. This was the start of the Special Air Service and it was to become a unit more feared by the Germans and Italians in the Western Desert than any other. In their heavily armed jeeps they ranged far behind the enemy lines, shooting up airfields and convoys and generally disrupting the enemy's lines of communications.

One of their most daring raids was the attack on Sidi Haneish, one moonlight night in August 1942. Sidi Haneish was one of the Germans' main staging aerodromes in the Western Desert and it was far behind the front line. Eighteen jeeps, in formation, raced into the aerodrome and, making a sweep right round the perimeter of the airfield, shot up every plane in sight.

Leaving the airfield blazing they raced back into the desert, leaving a completely demoralised enemy behind them. For the loss of two jeeps they had destroyed between forty and fifty German aircraft.

Peake was in trouble with the referee — but the Westford forward wanted his own justice!

through the players' tunnel for a much-needed breather.

"Some game," I grunted to Les Reid as we sat in our room drinking a quick cup of tea.

"Aye," he said. "I reckon if Denton stand much closer to Westford they'll be playing behind them!"

"Watch out for the fireworks in the next half," said Dave Christie, who was a born pessimist.

Boos And Bottles

WESTFORD came out for the second half in a clean strip. It was a case of "as you were" for the Denton boys. I suppose with having black shirts they thought it didn't really matter.

Within a few minutes the players were almost unrecognisable again as the batle in the mud continued. Jack Langan must have had a pep-talk with his lads during the interval, because they refused to be bogged down by the Denton tactics, and kept the ball moving around.

They almost scored on two occasions, but each time a player dropped the slippery ball with the line at his mercy. It looked as though the Rovers were losing their grip on the game and they began to show signs of weariness.

That's when they really started to get rough! Twice I had to haul Bull Blunden, the huge seventeen-stone prop forward, out of the scrum for using his fists. I had Plug Palmer on the carpet, too.

Then a burst of forward play left Roberts, the Westford hooker, rolling over and over in the mud in agony. I was unsighted by a ruck of players, but Les Reid came steaming on to the field with his flag raised.

"Peake struck him in the face after he'd parted with the ball," said Les harshly.

I called the burly Denton hooker over, but before he reached me, an incensed Westford forward, Flanagan, went for him. They struck out at each other, and members of their own sides dragged them apart.

I signalled on the Westford trainer to attend to Roberts, and proceeded to read the riot act to both sides. They got it hot and strong. Any more, and it would be a case of marching orders. Both the

names of Peake and Flanagan wen into my little black book.

The crowd were baying fo blood. Roberts regained his fee and I ordered a scrum. There was sudden upheaval as the two pack clashed. Peake had let fly at Robert again. Right under my nose !

I hauled the Denton hooker ou and pointed to the tunnel.

"You're finished," I snarled "Get off !"

As luck would have it, th incident occurred right under th shadow of the notorious east sid stand. When the old guard saw Peake slouching sullenly off, the went mad.

A hail of missiles showere around us and a bottle narrowl shaved Les Reid's ear. The polic had to go in amongst them, and was several minutes before w were able to get on with th game.

With Casey taking over the hook ing job, and Dent Dixon movin into the front row, the Rove packed only five forwards. The were still heavy enough to hold thei own in the pushing, but Case was consistently out-hooked b Roberts.

Hooking is a very specialise

...b, and I didn't envy Casey his ...ask against the best hooker in the ...ame.

Without the ball, Denton were ...orely handicapped, and Westford ...egan to give them the run around. ...ack Langan was playing a real ...aptain's game and was the main-...pring of nearly every movement.

Yet although the league leaders ...hipped the ball from man to man ...ith bewildering precision, a com-...ination of mud, bad luck, and ...lucky if ferocious Denton tackling ...ept the home side's line intact.

With five minutes to go it began ... look odds on a replay on the ...Vestford ground. By now the ...Vestford side were leg-weary, too, ...nd the close Denton marking had ...hem slogging away in the thick ...iud on the home side's twenty-...ve line.

But once again the irrepressible ...ack Langan tried to open the game ...ut and rally his men. Taking a pass on the burst from a play-the-ball, he sliced through dangerously, easily evading the clutching hands of Plug Palmer.

Losing his temper completely—and perhaps panicking at the thought of Langan going over under the sticks for the winning try, Palmer stuck out his foot and brought Langan down flat on his face.

As the Westford skipper writhed on the ground, I rushed over to Palmer and grabbed him by the arm.

"Off," I rasped angrily, pointing to the stand.

It was a stupid foul and one of the most dangerous in the book. It's the easiest way of breaking a player's leg I know. If it hadn't been for the fact that Langan had still to get round the full-back, I should have awarded an obstruction try.

Palmer didn't argue, but the rest of his side did. I pushed them angrily away, and to give the dismissed skipper credit, he told them to get on with the game before he left.

Although the Westford skipper's leg didn't appear to be broken, he was obviously going to be out of action for some time. The crowd were still booing my decision when he hobbled off on his trainer's arm.

Meanwhile Lacey, the Westford full-back, was wiping the mud off the toe of his boot prior to taking the penalty kick I had awarded.

It was right under the sticks, and would have been a certainty on a dry day. Even now, it wasn't a difficult shot to a kicker of Lacey's skill, but the noise from the crowd was terrific. The critical state of the game didn't help, either.

I motioned for Lacey to take the kick, and the crowd quietened as he poised at the beginning of his short run. But all of us on the field knew what was coming.

As he moved forward, the jeers and boos rose to a howling crescendo. Even so, they couldn't stop Lacey from putting the ball clean between the sticks to give Westford a 7-5 lead with minutes to go.

"Get Whistling Willie!"

FROM the kick-off, the Denton side made one desperate effort to pull the game out of the fire. With the crowd howling them on, their eleven men tore into the Westford team like fighting furies.

Westford were now content to hold out and defended grimly. If they could have got hold of the ball they would have kept it close till the final whistle.

Ironically enough, Denton started to play really open rugby in an attempt to find a way through. Time after time they were brought down inches from the line. They thoroughly deserved to score.

We were now playing in injury time, and I was almost ready to blow the final whistle. Suddenly Dent Dixon, the Denton second-row man, fielded a wild miskick

Lacey was trying for the winner and the crowd wanted him to miss!

from Lacey on the Westford twenty-five line, and, clutching the ball to his broad chest, set off on a powerful burst.

He shrugged aside one tackle, sold a beautiful dummy to another defender and put his head back with ten yards to go for the line.

Topping, the defending right-winger, came hurtling across to nail him. The wingman took off in a tremendous dive for the Denton man's legs.

But Dixon dived, too! Right up into the air and down again in a soaring arc that took him over Topping's outstretched figure and over the Westford line.

The ground literally exploded. Dixon was swamped with his own jubilant team-mates. Hats were flung into the air. Rattles sounded.

It was the worst moment of my life, disallowing that try.

As he fell, Dixon had dropped the ball over the line. Only a few inches perhaps, but enough to rule a score out. The ball must be grounded properly.

For a moment there was an ominous hush when it was seen that the try had been disallowed. Probably only myself and Dixon, if he was honest enough to admit it to himself, knew that there had been no score.

I was surrounded by players from both sides as I sounded the whistle for time. The Denton players were trying to get to me, and the Westford players were doing their best to keep them off.

My two linesmen, sensing trouble, rushed over to my side. The crowd were going crazy, and the police were scrambling over the rails to form a protective cordon. Rival supporters fought bitterly.

Then came the ominous cry, "Get Whistling Willie!" I can hear it yet.

As I walked slowly towards the dark opening of the tunnel in that east side stand, the ground suddenly went quiet. It was worse than the noise—a baleful, malevolent sort of silence, full of hatred.

A harassed police inspector came out to meet me.

"It's no use trying to get down the tunnel yet," he gasped. "We've sent for reinforcements! I've never seen a crowd in such an ugly mood!"

Now, I do not claim to be a hero. And I'm not a coward, either—cowards don't make good referees. But I knew if I went off that ground beneath a protective screen of players and police, I should never feel the same again.

I was confident that if I went off on my own, reason would prevail. The sight of the police clustered around me would only antagonise the crowd further.

Tearing myself away from the inspector I headed for the tunnel. Les Reid and Dave Christie were fairly close behind me, although I didn't realise it at the time.

As I reached the gate, I suddenly didn't feel so sure about the crowd's better judgment prevailing. I nearly turned back, but it was to late. I had to go on.

I almost pulled it off. Gazing straight ahead, I passed the rows of sullen faces until I had almost reached the tunnel mouth. A few more paces—then.

A huge angry man in a black and white scarf leapt over the fence and stood in my path. He was clutching a heavy rattle.

"Here," he shouted, brandish-ing the rattle menacingly, "wh are we waiting for?"

What indeed? Another ma scrambled over and joined him They moved forward menacingly I suddenly felt very small an helpless as the silence gave wa to tumult.

For a moment, my life was in th balance. I couldn't retreat, eithe because I could sense that othe hot-heads had climbed the fenc and were between the police and

Then two muddy figures emerge from the tunnel and grabbed th men who barred my path. I coul hardly recognise them at first, unt I saw they were Plug Palmer an Peake, the two players I had ser off.

The man swung his rattle an Palmer's huge fist took him clea on the chin. He collapsed in a hea and was joined a second later b the other spectator who collecte an uppercut from the Dento hooker.

Suddenly the tension snappe and common sense reigned agai Some of the spectators nearest th tunnel recognised the Dento captain and gave him a cheer.

The cheering spread to all par of the ground, and when the playe of both sides went down the tunn the bad feeling was gone, dispelle by the courageous action of tw local players.

I shook hands with the pair late in the dressing-room.

"Thanks, lads," I said thank fully. "I'll see that this is men tioned when my report goes in."

"Garn," said Plug Palmer wit a grin. "'Twern't nothing, re They just wanted to take you t have your eyes tested!"

I hadn't the heart to book him

THE END

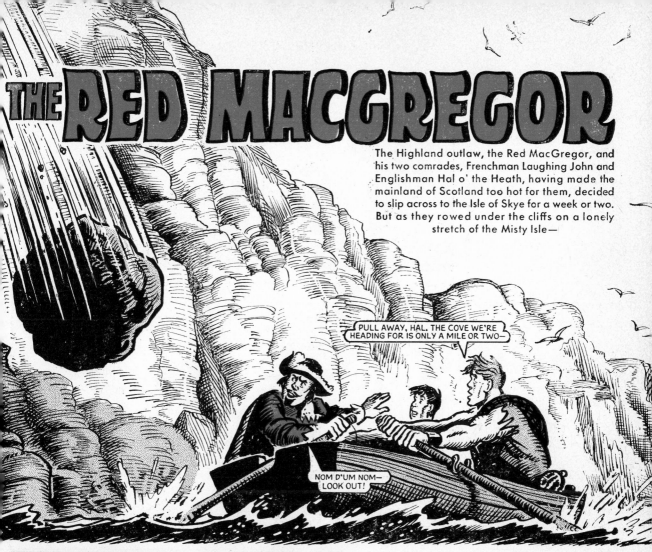

THE RED MACGREGOR

The Highland outlaw, the Red MacGregor, and his two comrades, Frenchman Laughing John and Englishman Hal o' the Heath, having made the mainland of Scotland too hot for them, decided to slip across to the Isle of Skye for a week or two. But as they rowed under the cliffs on a lonely stretch of the Misty Isle—

PULL AWAY, HAL, THE COVE WE'RE HEADING FOR IS ONLY A MILE OR TWO—

NOM D'UM NOM— LOOK OUT!

THAT BOULDER FALLING WAS NO ACCIDENT! SOMEONE UP THERE DOESN'T LIKE US!

AYE, JOHN! ROW FOR YOUR LIFE, HAL!

THAT'S A STRANGE WELCOME TO GET FROM THE MEN OF SKYE! WHAT'S TO BE DONE NOW? WE MUST HAVE SOME FOOD AND WATER AND WE CAN'T RETURN TO THE MAINLAND.

WHY DID THEY ATTACK US? THEY DON'T KNOW WHO WE ARE. IF THEY THINK THEY CAN STOP US LANDING, THEY'LL HAVE TO BE TAUGHT DIFFERENTLY. PULL FOR THE COVE, HAL.

IT'S NO USE. THOSE FELLOWS ARE FOLLOWING ROUND THE CLIFFS. THEY'LL WRECK US FOR SURE IF WE TRY TO PULL IN.

WILL THEY? LOOK, THEY'LL HAVE TO GO BEHIND THAT OUTCROP OF ROCK IN A MINUTE. THAT MEANS WE'LL BE OUT OF THEIR SIGHT FOR A SHORT WHILE. THAT GIVES ME AN IDEA.

WHEN THEY COME BACK INTO SIGHT OF THE BOAT, A PLAID ON YOUR STAFF WILL MAKE THEM THINK THERE'S STILL THREE OF US IN THE BOAT BUT I'LL BE SWIMMING ASHORE UNDER WATER. TAKE BOTH OARS, HAL, AND KEEP PULLING.

The islanders were out of sight for several minutes behind the outcrop and before they reappeared, the Red MacGregor had swum well inshore. The men never noticed how they were being tricked by the dummy of the plaid and the stick. The MacGregor landed, climbed the cliff and was soon at the top behind the two islanders.

CAUGHT YOU, MY BEAUTIES! I'LL TEACH YOU TO THROW ROCKS AT A MACGREGOR AND HIS FRIENDS!

THAT'LL COOL THE PAIR OF YOU OFF, AND MAKE YOU MORE READY TO ANSWER QUESTIONS WHEN I GET DOWN THERE!

NAME OF A CROSS-EYED MULE! I HOPE YOU GENTLEMEN ENJOYED YOUR BATHE. NOW WE'LL TAKE YOU ASHORE AND GET AN EXPLANATION FROM YOU.

THROWING ROCKS—WHAT WAY WAS THAT TO GREET THE RED MACGREGOR AND HIS FRIENDS?

YOU'RE THE RED MACGREGOR—THE OUTLAW? WE DIDN'T KNOW. WE THOUGHT YOU AND YOUR COMRADES WERE SOME OF THE BLACK COLONEL'S MEN.

WHO IS THE BLACK COLONEL AND WHAT HAVE YOU GOT AGAINST HIM AND HIS MEN?

WHO IS THE BLACK COLONEL? MAY THE CURSE OF FINGAL BE UPON HIM. HE IS THE REDCOAT OFFICER WHO ORDERED THE MASSACRE OF THE MACIANS. OUR OWN CHIEF WAS TAKEN AWAY BY HIM TO LONDON AND HANGED FOR TAKING PART IN THE RISING OF THE CLANS. AS A REWARD THE GOVERNMENT GRANTED THE BLACK COLONEL THE ISLE OF SKYE.

THE BLACK COLONEL'S GOING TO TURN SKYE INTO A PLACE FOR SPORTSMEN. HE IS DRIVING THE PEOPLE OF SKYE FROM THEIR CROFTS AND MEANS TO SHIP THEM IN CHAINS TO AMERICA. WHEN WE'VE ALL BEEN CLEARED OFF, HE'S GOING TO STOCK THE ISLAND WITH GAME FOR HIS GUESTS TO SHOOT AT!

THE COLONEL'S SHIP'S IN THE HARBOUR AT DHEARG NOW. SOME OF US HAVE GONE INTO HIDING BUT THEY'RE HUNTING US ALL OVER THE ISLAND

COME, WE WILL GO TO DHEARG AND SEE WHAT IS TO BE DONE!

Two hours later.

MAY THE CURSE OF FINGAL BE ON YOU AND YOURS FOREVER, YOU BLACK FIEND!

SO THAT ONE ON THE HORSE IS THE BLACK COLONEL, EH?

Captured!

The death of the Black Colonel!

AAAARGH!

I SEE YOU ARE UNARMED, GENTLEMEN. UNLESS YOU WISH TO SHARE THE COLONEL'S FATE, I ADVISE YOU TO TRY NO TRICKS. I AM LEAVING NOW.

Next day—

THE REDCOATS SPENT A FRUIT-LESS NIGHT COMBING THE ISLAND FOR ME. NOW THE GOVERNMENT SHIP HAS COME TO TAKE THEM AWAY.

THAT SHOULD HOLD THEM TILL I GET SAFELY AWAY.

When the government ship had left, the slave ship returned. MacGregor went out to her.

GO BACK TO YOUR HOMES, MEN OF SKYE. THE REDCOATS HAVE GONE AND THE BLACK COLONEL IS DEAD. HAL, FETCH THE CAPTAIN. I WANT A WORD WITH HIM.

AYE, AYE, MACGREGOR.

CAPTAIN, WHEN THE ISLANDERS ARE ALL ASHORE, TAKE YOUR SHIP AND YOUR MEN AWAY. THEY ARE NOT NEEDED HERE NOW. WHEN YOU MAKE YOUR REPORT, I TRUST YOU, AS AN HONOURABLE MAN, TO SAY THAT THE RED MACGREGOR ALONE WAS RESPONSIBLE FOR THE MUTINY AND THAT NO VENGEANCE CAN BE JUSTLY TAKEN ON INNOCENT ISLES FOLK.

YES, THAT WILL BE COMMON HONESTY. AND WE'LL SHAKE HANDS ON IT. YOU MAY BE AN OUTLAW AND A MACGREGOR, BUT, SHIVER MY TIMBERS, YOU'RE A MAN!

THE END

WINGED WATCH-DOGS OF UCHIZA PASS

Reg Wilde operated an air delivery service high amongst the Andes mountains in Peru. He often had to fly through Uchiza Pass when delivering medical supplies to the mining town of Salonte, but this was dangerous. Vicious eagles nested in the pass and attacked anything that flew. Repeated complaints to the Peruvian Government that something should be done had brought no satisfaction—and now Reg was being attacked again . . .

HERE'S THOSE DARNED EAGLES AGAIN. THIS IS WHERE MY JOB BECOMES TRICKY.

FOOLED YOU THAT TIME, MY FEATHERED FRIENDS.

THE STUPID BIRDS THINK THAT THIS PLANE IS ANOTHER KIND OF BIRD WHICH IS TRYING TO TAKE OVER THEIR LAND, I BET.

THEY WON'T BOTHER ABOUT ME NOW BECAUSE I'M GETTING OUT OF THEIR TERRITORY.

Departure to danger!

SALONTE AT LAST!

AH, SENOR WILDE. I TRUST YOU HAD A PLEASANT TRIP.

IT WASN'T GOOD, FERNANDEZ, BUT IT COULD HAVE BEEN A LOT WORSE.

WHO ARE THESE PEOPLE AND WHY ARE THEY PRISONERS?

THEY ARE JIVAROS. THEY COME TO THIS PART OF THE WORLD LOOKING FOR SLAVES, AND THEY FIND THE MENA TRIBESMEN VERY EASY TARGETS FOR THEIR TRADING.

I DIDN'T THINK THAT SORT OF THING STILL WENT ON.

Soon the medical supplies were unloaded from Reg's plane . . .

GOODBYE, SENOR WILDE, I HOPE YOU HAVE A SAFE JOURNEY BACK TO LIMA.

OH YES, SENOR. SLAVE TRADING AMONGST THESE LOCAL TRIBESMEN HAS BEEN GOING ON FOR MANY, MANY YEARS. THEY WERE THE SLAVES OF THE FAMOUS INCAS AND THEIR WHOLE TRADITION HAS BEEN ONE OF SLAVERY. IT IS SAID THAT THE MENA TRIBESMEN WERE THE ONES WHO HID THE FAMOUS INCA TREASURE TROVES IN CAVES IN MOUNTAINS. WHETHER THERE IS ANY TRUTH TO THAT RUMOUR I DO NOT KNOW.

I HOPE SO TOO. IT ALL DEPENDS ON ONE OR TWO BIRDS.

LIMA HERE I COME!

NO SIGN OF THE EAGLES YET.

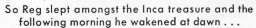

So Reg slept amongst the Inca treasure and the following morning he wakened at dawn . . .

77

"I was lucky to get away with my life."

THIS SHOULD FETCH ENOUGH MONEY TO BUY ME A NEW PLANE. A HELICOPTER WOULD BE BEST BECAUSE NOTHING ELSE WOULD BE ABLE TO LAND ON THE LEDGE OUTSIDE. THEN I CAN TRANSPORT THE STUFF AWAY, SELL IT, AND BE ONE OF THE RICHEST MEN IN THE WORLD.

MY FIRST JOB WILL BE TO CLIMB DOWN THAT PRECIPICE TO THE FLOOR OF THE VALLEY. IT'S NOT GOING TO BE EASY.

Reg was right. The climb down the cliff was not easy and it took him a long time. His troubles weren't over when he reached the bottom either, because he had a long, perilous journey ahead of him—a journey which took him some days. Then one day in the middle of the afternoon . . .

. . . Reg saw a sight which gladdened his heart!

PEOPLE! THANK GOODNESS! I THOUGHT I'D NEVER MAKE IT.

AH! YOU MUST BE SENOR WILDE. WE HAVE BEEN SEARCHING FOR YOU. SOME LOCAL VILLAGERS SAW SMOKE FROM YOUR PLANE AND FEARED THE WORST. WE THOUGHT YOU HAD PERISHED.

I COULD HAVE PERISHED QUITE EASILY. MY PLANE WAS ATTACKED BY A COUPLE OF EAGLES—EAGLES THAT I HAVE COMPLAINED ABOUT BEFORE. MAYBE THEY'LL TAKE SOME ACTION THIS TIME. BUT I DOUBT IT.

Eventually Reg got back to Lima, the capital of Peru. There he had an interview with a Government official, but Reg knew how these interviews went—he'd had them before.

I'VE COMPLAINED ABOUT THESE EAGLES BEFORE! NOTHING'S BEEN DONE AND NOW I'VE HAD A CRASH BECAUSE MY PLANE WAS ATTACKED BY THEM. I WAS LUCKY TO GET AWAY WITH MY LIFE. PERHAPS YOU'LL DO SOMETHING NOW, ALTHOUGH I DOUBT IT. IT WOULD NEED ONE OF THE PLANES IN THE PERUVIAN AIR FORCE TO BE ATTACKED BEFORE ANYTHING WOULD BE DONE.

I AM SORRY, SENOR WILDE. IT'S A PITY ABOUT YOUR PLANE! I SHALL PUT YOUR COMPLAINT THROUGH THE PROPER CHANNELS.

As soon as Reg left the Government office he made straight for a back street jeweller he had heard of . . .

HOW MUCH FOR THIS LOT?

IT IS OF GOOD QUALITY AND VERY OLD. I WILL GIVE YOU THREE HUNDRED THOUSAND SOLS. THAT IS ABOUT THREE THOUSAND POUNDS IN BRITISH MONEY.

"What on earth are they doing up there?"

"I'd better get out of here quick!"

THERE'S SOME PLANES UP THERE BUT I'M NOT IN THEIR WAY AT ALL.

GREAT GRIEF! THEY'RE DROPPING BOMBS!

CRUMBS! THOSE BOMBS HAVEN'T HALF STARTED SOMETHING—I'D BETTER GET OUT OF HERE QUICK!

OH, NO! IT WOULD REQUIRE DOZENS OF BULLDOZERS AND MONTHS OF HARD LABOUR TO CLEAR THAT LOT AWAY. THE TREASURE FOUND JUST WOULDN'T BE WORTH IT. IT WOULD COST AS MUCH TO FINANCE THE WHOLE OPERATION.

AND THERE ARE THOSE BLASTED EAGLES UNHARMED. THEIR NESTS HAVE BEEN DESTROYED BUT NOT THEM. THEY'RE JUST LAUGHING AT ME. I'VE GOT A HELICOPTER NOW INSTEAD OF AN AUSTER, BUT I'M REALLY RIGHT BACK WHERE I STARTED!

WHAT'S WRONG WITH HOT-SHOT HALL?

HI, THERE! MY NAME IS BILL POWELL AND I'M CHIEF SCOUT FOR BURNHAM CITY, ONE OF THE TOP CLUBS IN THE FIRST DIVISION. OTHER CLUBS ALSO HAVE SCOUTS AND THIS MEANS I'VE ALWAYS TO BE A STEP AHEAD OF THEM TO LAND A GOOD PLAYER. I OFTEN HAVE TO GO TO A LOT OF TROUBLE TO LAND A PLAYER. SOMETIMES IT'S WORTH IT AND OTHERS IT ISN'T. ONE DAY I WENT TO WATCH JIMMY HALL, AN INSIDE-FORWARD, WHO PLAYED FOR FORDHAM CITY, A LOWLY THIRD DIVISION CLUB.

I was not alone in my interest in a Fordham player. Fred Phillips, the scout for Carford City, was there.

HALLO, BILL, HOW ARE YOU DOING?

I'M FINE, FRED. ARE YOU HERE TO SEE ANYONE IN PARTICULAR?

NO, NO. JUST LOOKING AROUND. HOW ABOUT YOU?

OH, JUST THE SAME, FRED, NOBODY IN PARTICULAR.

The players came out and the game started. Jimmy Hall was playing at inside-left.

82

E, THAT SUPPORTER'S
T HIS HEAD SCREWED
N ALL RIGHT. IT WAS A
AND GOAL AND JIMMY
HALL MADE IT.

That was the only goal until five minutes from the final whistle when Fordham got a corner.

GREAT GOAL, JIMMY. YOU POSITIONED YOURSELF WELL THERE!

The final whistle went then, but I'd seen enough!

I'D BETTER SEE THE MANAGER.

But Fred beat me to it!

WE'RE QUITE WILLING TO TRANSFER JIMMY BUT IT'S UP TO HIM IF HE WANTS TO GO.

I'LL NIP ALONG TO THE DRESSING ROOMS AND CATCH JIMMY HALL THERE.

DIRECTORS R

83

Such was the layout of the course that once we started we had to go over every obstacle.

"This lad is as good as any I've ever signed."

MADE IT!

UGH!

I'VE COME TO ASK YOU TO SIGN FOR BURNHAM CITY, BUT I MUST TELL YOU THAT CARFORD CITY ARE ALSO AFTER YOU. FRED, THERE, IS WITH THEM!

BURNHAM! COR, I'VE ALWAYS WANTED TO PLAY FOR YOU. I'LL SIGN RIGHT AWAY IF IT'S ALL RIGHT WITH FORDHAM.

RIGHT THEN, WE'LL FIX THINGS AND YOU CAN COME AND SEE ME. I'LL GIVE YOU MY ADDRESS.

RIGHT YOU ARE, I'LL SEE YOU!

COR! ALL THAT FOR NOTHING. STILL, THAT'S FOOTBALL.

We pushed Jimmy's transfer throug[h] and when he was demobbed I too[k] him along to see Dave Main, th[e] manager of Burnham City.

COR, IT AIN'T HALF BIG. THIS MAKES OLD FORDHAM'S GROUND SEEM TINY.

AYE IT'S BIG ENOUGH, BUT THEY'RE A RIGHT FRIENDLY CROWD HERE. COME ON IN AND I'LL INTRODUCE YOU TO DAVE MAIN.

DAVE, THIS IS JIMMY HALL, THE YOUNG LAD I WAS TELLING YOU ABOUT.

GLAD TO MEET YOU, SON. COME UP TO THE OFFICE AND WE'LL HAVE A CHAT. SEE YOU LATER, BILL.

Later . . .

I'M THINKING OF PLAYING HIM IN THE FIRST TEAM ON SATURDAY, BILL. WE'VE HAD A LOT OF TROUBLE WITH THE INSIDE-LEFT POSITION. WHAT DO YOU THINK, IS HE UP TO IT?

I TELL YOU, DAVE, THIS LAD IS AS GOOD AS ANY I'VE EVER SIGNED.

RIGHT, THAT'S GOOD ENOUGH FOR ME, BILL. IF YOU SAY HE'S A GOOD 'UN, HE'LL BE A GOOD 'UN. HE'S PLAYING ON SATURDAY.

"He's a right dumpling."

That Saturday Jimmy lined up with the rest of the Burnham team against Grafton Rovers.

THERE YOU ARE, JIMMY.

COR, WHAT'S THIS WE'VE GOT? HE'S A RIGHT DUMPLING.

OH NO, I'VE STARTED OFF BADLY.

Jimmy had a terrible game and Burnham lost 3-1. After the game I was collared by Dave Main.

WHAT'S THIS THEN, BILL? YOU SAID THIS LAD WAS A GOOD 'UN.

WELL I TELL YOU, DAVE, WHEN I SAW HIM PLAY HE WAS A WORLD BEATER. GIVE HIM ANOTHER CHANCE NEXT WEEK. HE MIGHT HAVE JUST HAD AN OFF DAY.

OKAY THEN, BILL, I'LL TRUST YOU. BUT IF HE PLAYS LIKE THAT NEXT WEEK HE'S HAD HIS CHIPS FOR SOME TIME AS FAR AS FIRST DIVISION FOOTBALL IS CONCERNED.

OKAY, DAVE, THAT'S FAIR ENOUGH.

The following week we were playing away against Marbridge Town, a lowly First Division club, whose ground was quite near Fordham City's.

I HOPE JIMMY PLAYS BETTER THIS WEEK. IT'S STARTING TO LOOK LIKE THAT BLOKE AT THE CAMP WAS RIGHT!

COR, I'VE STARTED OFF AS BADLY AS LAST WEEK. I JUST CAN'T GET SETTLED.

"You're playing like a novice."

Jimmy's first half was a disaster! Coming out for the second half—

COME ON, JIMMY, YOU'RE PLAYING LIKE A NOVICE. LET'S SEE YOU DO SOMETHING NOW.

IT'S YOU, ALF! THAT MAKES ME FEEL MORE AT HOME.

A few minutes later

ONLY ONE MORE TO GO THEN I'LL SHOW THEM.

A GOAL! JIMMY'S PLAYING BETTER. I THINK I KNOW WHAT WAS WRONG WITH HIM.

Jimmy played a binder to help us win 3-0.

RACE TO WYATT'S FERRY

AXEL THORSEN and his crew of four Laplanders were wanderers of the Arctic Circle.

In all his thirty years Axel had never dwelt in a house, though he was rich enough to have owned the finest house in the Yukon. The only dwelling he wanted was his tent of caribou hide.

Every year he travelled more than a thousand miles on foot in the latitude of the Arctic Circle, following his ever-growing herd of 800 caribou, the deer of northernmost Canada.

Axel, a Laplander himself, had been born in a tent in Arctic Norway, born to this roaming life of deer herding. As a young man he had emigrated with four friends to Canada. Up on the head-waters of Peel River, in Yukon territory, they had trapped silver foxes for a while, then one day they had sighted a vast herd of caribou roaming free, owned by no man. Axel had a great idea.

Here were their " cattle," and the entire territory of Arctic Canada could be their " ranch " —all for the taking. He and his pals grasped their opportunity. Using the herding methods for reindeer that they had learnt so thoroughly in Lapland, they managed to cut off 300 of the little antlered beasts from the fleeing multitude and corral them in a mountain canyon.

Each of these five " cowboys on foot " lassoed for himself a promising-looking buck and proceeded to break it to harness use. They taught the deer to draw their sleds—at a faster pace than any sled-dogs. Thus equipped, they were able to

A life or death race in the frozen wastes of Canada.

ride around their herd and keep it together. And within a few months the reindeer were so accustomed to their herders they no longer bolted at the sight of them. They were becoming as domesticated as cattle.

Unlike ranch cattle, however, they could never settle in one region. It was their nature to roam afar, from one feeding ground to another, grazing the nutritive grass in the summer, browsing off thick tree moss in snow seasons.

And the herders, understanding their natures, had to roam with them. Instead of ruling their herd they were ruled by these docile little beasts. It was the only way to keep them flourishing. The herd was their meat and milk supply, their clothing and transportation.

Axel was the business head of this little ranching venture. It was he who obtained a contract to supply quantities of deer meat to a Dawson butcher—who shipped it south at a fat profit and sold it in the Alberta cities as prime venison. Every year at the beginning of autumn, Axel drove his herd to a point on the Yukon River where the butcher met him with a convoy of great waggons. The meat was slaughtered then and there and was paid for.

Year by year the Thorsen herd grew and was added to, as opportunity offered, by fresh captures from wild herds. Axel and his partners became prosperous, and they wouldn't have swopped their roaming lives and skin tents for a king's palace. Other men envied them their wealth and tried to gather herds of their own. But they never succeeded as the Laplanders, who knew the job so completely. They couldn't lasso, couldn't break in the deer, and tried to force unnatural feeding habits on the beasts. Their herds dwindled

The Crow Indians were in a desperate situation — Tom Price's store was burning down, and it contained the only food for one hundred miles.

instead of growing, and hordes of ravenous wolves killed off scores at each lightning raid. That never happened with alert Axel Thorsen and his partners, who were always sharp-eyed for any signs of wolves or catamounts in the vicinity, and fought many a battle against these fierce marauders.

A Desperate Journey

ONE hundred miles north of Dawson, just "under the Arctic Circle," was the Circle Fur Trading Post, owned by Tom Price.

The white trappers and Indians came to Tom every November when the first snow had fallen, and he allowed them, on credit, a winter stock of food supplies and traps. In spring they brought their furs to him, and, after deducting what they owed him, he paid them a cash balance for their catches.

This particular autumn, calamity struck at the Circle Post, which was fully stocked with its winter merchandise. A few days after the first heavy snowfall the big heating furnace in the basement—which kept stocks from freezing on the store shelves—exploded. The big store, with its entire stock in trade, was burned to the ground.

The dozens of Indian families encamped near the store, who had been about to draw their winter rations from Tom, were in a desperate plight. Most of them were at starvation point. Knowing they could have as much food on credit as they required from the trader, they had recklessly used up all their remaining stocks.

Now they had nothing left, and there was nothing salvaged from the fire. There was no food for this crowd of fifty-odd Indian bucks, their squaws, and small, hungry children—no food for one hundred miles. Eagle Pass was the nearest town, from which Tom had packed in his supplies. And 200 miles to Eagle Pass and back was a journey of many days, in present deep snow conditions.

Tom Price had an almost fatherly affection for these Indians. He pitied them in their plight and decided to make the journey. He owned the champion dog-sled team of the Yukon—five splendid curly-tailed malemutes. They had won many a hundred dollars for him at the Dawson Dog-Sled Trials.

He harnessed his famous malemute team and promised the Indians he would be back with the supplies in one week. It was a tremendous promise to make, but if his dogs could put up as grand a performance as they had in the Trials, he would make it—or bust.

The King Caribou

NOT only these lowly Crow Indians were depending on the Circle Store. Axel Thorsen, whose caribou herd was browsing in the Porcupine Forest twenty miles to the north, was driving in to the store for supplies.

Axel and Tom Price were great friends, though there was one subject on which they never could agree. Tom was all for dog teams drawing sleds. Axel was all for deer. Axel maintained that a caribou could haul a load of 200 pounds, and cover, if necessary, 100 miles in twenty-four hours, whereas it took a big dog to haul 70 pounds and thirty miles a day was its limit.

"Sure, sure," Tom would snort. "But a caribou is three times as big as a dog. With a three-dog team I could——"

"You could haul as big a load—maybe! But you couldn't go as fast and as far, Tom. And my deer, with their spreading cloven hooves, like snowshoes, can travel in soft snow that would bog down your small-pawed dogs."

They always argued, but good-humouredly. Axel, the Laplander, had always been used to deer in

of sleigh bells on the deer's harness.

Axel got a shock. There was no familiar store—just an ugly pile of black, smouldering ashes in the snow. That friendly log store, like a great treasure-chest crammed with everything of interest to a man of the wilds, was all gone up in smoke and flames. And there, in the midst of a crowd of dejected Indians, was Tom Price with his famous dog-sled all ready for a journey.

The two friends discussed the calamity.

"Yep, I'm fully covered by insurance," assured Tom. "But these hungry Injuns can't eat

who were staring at him dejectedly. He told them he still had a small stock of rice, flour, beans, and tea, and there was all the deer meat they could eat, and milk for their babies. If they would trek 20 miles to Porcupine Creek they could eat on the "Thorsen Ranch" till Tom got back.

The Indians were grateful, and Tom admired Axel more than ever. Few men would have fed such a multitude of hungry mouths for a week, and free of charge. But this big blond-haired Laplander was a true man of the north. He would share his last crust with a fellow man in need.

Most men rode on dog-sleds in northernmost Canada — but not Axel Thorsen. His sled was pulled by Haakon, the king caribou.

sleds—Tom to malemutes and husky dogs. Neither could convince the other.

On this occasion Axel came driving into the store clearing with Haakon, the king caribou of his herd. Haakon was a magnificent twelve-point buck, light-brown on top, dark-brown underneath, and so tall for a caribou that its shoulders were as high as Axel's broad chest, and Axel was a six-footer.

Axel, in very soft snow, preferred a long, flat-bottomed toboggan with a curled-up forward end. Haakon could pull this light rig, which skimmed over the surface without sinking, at a tremendous speed. He came flashing into the clearing now with a lively jingle

insurance money. It's stocks I need for them. And I'm heading for Eagle Pass right now. I can carry back enough to keep them eating for a month. And I'll fix it for more supplies to be coming along."

"Look, Tom," suggested Axel, as concerned about the Crows as Tom was. "Let me go instead. I'll get there quicker."

"What—with that flimsy toboggan which couldn't carry two hundredweight aboard it? No, sir, I'll go."

Axel offered to harness Haakon to Tom's larger freight sled, which had deep, steel-shod runners. But Tom wouldn't listen. He would be back in a week, he bragged—or bust the sled traces trying.

Axel then spoke to the Indians

Hi-Jacked!

SO Axel Thorsen fed the fifty-odd men, women, and children of the Crow tribe for a week in his little camp on Porcupine Creek, where the herd of thick-coated deer was browsing off the plentiful tree moss.

On the eighth day he set off with Haakon for a quick sled drive back to the black ruins of the Circle Store, to be sure Tom was back, before the Indians returned to him. But when Axel arrived there was no Tom Price. The place was bleak and deserted. It proved what Axel had contended, that Tom

Tom Price befriended three strangers on the trail — but they repaid him by knocking him out and stealing his vital supplies.

had gone west, and the three men on snowshoes, going at a jog-trot. But here were Tom Price's tracks—with the Star brand of his rubber boots in the snow—heading back down his previous day's trail, as if returning alone to Eagle Pass. Axel thrust his fingers in the grey ashes of the camp-fire. The ashes were cold.

With a definite fear for Tom's welfare, he leapt on his toboggan, gathered the reins, and barked a command to Haakon, who promptly bounded forward and went trotting away with him as fast as a Kentucky pacing horse on a racetrack. Axel drove him along Tom's trail, following his footprints.

He drove for a dozen miles before he sighted the lone figure ahead, plodding along under a sky that had in the last hour grown black and threatening, across a stretch of open tundra country. He knew it was Tom staggering wearily along over the deep snow, heading away from him. Axel cried out, and in the stillness of the snowy waste his shout carried to Tom, who spun around.

He almost collapsed in Axel's arms when the deer toboggan pulled up beside him.

" Axel," he groaned. " I was hijacked by three mangy coyotes !"

As he sat on Axel's toboggan, he showed the Laplander a black-bruised lump the size of a hen's egg above his temple.

" That's what I got for taking pity on hungry men," he said bitterly. He told how on his way to Eagle Pass he had met three wolf hunters camped in that pine grove. They seemed down on their luck and hungry. He had shared his supper with them. Incautiously he had told of his burned-out store, and how he was going for fresh supplies. On his return journey, they were still camped in the trees.

" They'd shot a deer, they claimed, and had been resting up and getting their fill of deer meat before moving on. But that was a lie, I believe. I believe they just hung around till I got back with my load. Then they palled up again—me supplying the supper again."

They had brought their bed-rolls and laid them down beside Tom's, telling him they were heading east next morning for the Peel River, where wolves abounded.

ouldn't make it in a week with a heavy load of stores.

Axel generously set off on the trail to Eagle Pass. He would meet Tom, and Haakon, with his great pulling power, would help pull the sled-load on the end of a long towing-line. He expected to meet Tom a few miles out. But he went ten miles without a sign of the trader.

After he had travelled twenty miles he came upon the signs of a camp in the shelter of a dark pine grove. Axel had no schooling. He could not read nor write. But he could read snow signs as others might read a story. These signs were as telling as a printed report to him.

Tom had reached this far on his return journey and had camped for the night at the edge of the trees. In among the trees were three other sets of prints, men on webbed snowshoes. These tracks joined up with Tom's. Evidently he had had the company of three other men. The marks of four blanket beds laid down on spruce boughs were imprinted in the snow.

But here was a queer thing ! On breaking camp, Tom had forsaken the northern trail to his Circle Store. He had headed west, with those men accompanying him. Now why was that ?

Suddenly Axel's trained eye saw something. The sled and dogs

Sometime before dawn Tom awoke to find one of the rascals kneeling over him, with his rifle-butt upraised. Before Tom could do anything, the iron-shod butt struck down, knocking him senseless in his bed. When he came-to, the men had gone, taking his champion malemute team and its three-hundredweight load of supplies.

"They went west, the dirty, lying coyotes," raged Tom. "But Ben Logan will get the skunks."

"The Mountie sergeant from Placer Bar?" asked Axel.

"Yep. He's expected in Eagle Pass any day, coming down the Yukon River, to issue trapping licences. There's a dozen trappers waiting for him. Maybe he's there right now. I'm heading there on chance."

you said. They'll be across the Yukon River on to American territory before you can see Logan."

The Chase!

TOM said nothing, but looked utterly hopeless. Young blond Axel Thorsen wasn't looking hopeless, however, he looked unusually stern and determined. While they had talked, an icy, moaning wind had risen. They knew it was the prelude to a blizzard.

"Hang on tight, Tom," Axel ordered suddenly. And gathering Haakon's reins he stepped aboard the toboggan. "Hi!" he barked, and the big reindeer lowered its

"You bet," Axel answered "We're going to get your load back. Those Crows need the grub in the worst way. And you'll nev be right again till you have you dogs back."

"You've said it, lad. But they've got three rifles. And, believe me they're just the villains who would use them on us."

"I've got my hunting rifle. I' use it on them—if they fire first There isn't a court in the North would blame me if I had to kil to stop such crooks. They've don a robbery with violence agains you. I know what Sergeant Loga would do if they fired on him. An if it's the duty of a Mountie t stop robbers, it's every good citizen's duty, too."

"I'm all for you, Axel. Bu

Axel Thorsen had made up his mind to catch the crooks—and not even a blizzard was going to stop him.

Axel shook his fair head, thoughtfully.

"It's my idea, Tom, that those hi-jackers are heading for parts where your malemute team isn't known—to sell the dogs and the grub, too. Everyone in the Yukon knows your team, but they're not known in Alaska. And the boundary line is only 70 miles west of here. Those robbers were heading west,

twelve-point antlers and leaned into the broad, rawhide breast-collar, then bounded forward. Instead of heading straight on for Eagle Pass, Axel made a wide turn, then veered off at an angle from the tracks he had made coming. He was heading north-west across the tundra.

"You're going to chase after them, Axel?" asked Tom.

we'll never sight them this side the Yukon. They've got six hour start on us."

"But I've got Haakon and th light toboggan. They're heav loaded. We'll catch up with the Tom—hi, Haakon!"

The deer was going like the win now, fairly skimming over th snow. The speed made the ic wind cut across Tom's cheekbon

Axel and Tom could see the crooks in the distance — but would they catch them before they reached the ferry?

They had come to the edge of a sheltering pine forest. In the blinding snow flurries Axel up-ended the toboggan, leaning it sloping from a great windfallen pine trunk, forming a low roof. He chopped fir and spruce boughs and laid them across it, then built a roaring fire. Finally, he tethered Haakon on a long rope so the deer could get at the tree moss. Then, with Axel's grub bag, the two men crawled into their shelter, blanketless.

Dawn came after a sleepless night. Though Axel had kept the fire blazing, they had been too numbed with cold to sleep. But, at any rate, the blizzard had blown itself out. And in the far distance was Sugarloaf Peak, its conical summit coloured pink by the rising sun. The Sugarloaf was a famous landmark, rising to 8000 feet, with the Yukon River and Wyatt's Ferry at its northern base.

After a breakfast of hardtack, bully beef, and strong black coffee, they set off in the piercing cold of sunrise. Axel drove Haakon—as white with plastered snow as a marble statue—at amazing speed over the blinding-white snow wastes.

By late afternoon he reckoned they had come fifty miles since the evening before, in spite of the blizzard, and were now climbing the foothills on the south side of the Sugarloaf.

They had not sighted a living thing in all that distance. Had their journey been for nothing? Had the runaways made off to some other destination? When they surmounted the lofty ridge seven miles ahead of them, they would have an uninterrupted view down the treeless slopes of the mountain, right to the river and the ferry. If any sled outfit was moving down these snowfields, they would be in full view. There was a small village at Wyatt's Ferry on the Canadian side of the river, dense forest on the Alaskan side.

They reached the ridge summit at last and Axel halted for the caribou to recover its wind. They could see the distant black line of the river and dark forest beyond. Ten miles to the north was the small collection of log cabins at the Ferry.

Suddenly Axel's sharp eyes saw a dark speck moving down the

ike whips of wire. Never had he travelled over the tundra at such an exhilarating pace.

If Axel's guess was right, and those robbers were planning to cross the Yukon River into Alaska, they would have to cross by Wyatt's Ferry, as the river wasn't yet frozen over. Axel was now heading directly across country for the ferry raft.

The runaways had six hours' start, plus the distance Axel had come out of his way to find Tom. They might make the ferry in two days, from where they had started. It seemed impossible to Tom Price that the deer could make it by then—seventy miles. But the young Laplander kept assuring him they had a chance. The robbers were heavy-laden, he said. Tom said the deer toboggan was heavy-laden, too, with two men aboard.

But Axel drove on, deaf to all arguments—until suddenly, at the

close of day, they ran head-on into the descending curtain of a roaring blizzard. Even then, though Haakon kept trying to turn his shoulder to it, to keep it from blinding him, Axel held him ruthlessly straight into the teeth of it. It was torment for the deer and for the two men, but head-on into the white storm was the direction they must keep, or be lost.

Long after darkness, since it was a treeless country, Axel held on to this course, encouraging the deer with loud shouts and rousing whipcracks. While Axel stood upright in the full blast, Tom crouched with his back to it on the toboggan's rear end. He was just a shapeless mound of fur plastered with driving snow, and was in danger of freezing stiff. It was Tom's weakness which made Axel come to a halt in the end, after many hours of forging through the stormy darkness.

north flank of the mountain. It was a sled outfit.

"There they are—sure as a gunshot," he cried. "They came around the north side. That's why we never sighted them." He gathered the reins and cracked his whip. Haakon, breathless as he was, got going at a spanking pace immediately.

"They've got four miles to go to the ferry—we've got ten," Axel grinned in triumph. "Travelling downhill, we can make it five times as fast as they can. You'll see—hi, Haakon!"

Tom said nothing, but hoped Axel was right. If the crooks beat them to the ferry raft, they could leave it over on the far side and Axel would have no means of crossing after them.

Downhill To Danger

IT was a vast relief to the king caribou to be going downhill after that long climb. He went at race-horse speed, his legs flashing underneath him with the speed of machinery.

The stolen five-dog sled was forced to labour, even on downhill going, for the runners sank so deep. But the toboggan skimmed over the fresh snow surface like racing skis. How right Axel had been, Tom was thinking. The deer was swooping down to the lower levels like a winged horse.

In a matter of minutes they were reaching a point on the snowy prairie level where they were coming between the oncoming sled and the ferry. Axel and Tom were both standing on the speeding toboggan, their arms flung up, both shouting across, commanding the

sled to stop. The robbers must have recognised Tom. They were desperate men. They had to get to the ferry raft before the whole village turned out to stop them. Once on the raft, hauling themselves across by the cable, they could cut the haul-back line and get clear away into the forest with no fear of pursuit.

They were determined not to be taken. One of them fell to one knee in the snow. His rifle cracked. The bullet whistled close over Haakon. Axel's jaw set like a steel trap. They were going to slay Haakon, so that the toboggan would be brought to a halt.

"Here, Tom, you take the lines." He thrust the reins into Tom's hand and picked up his rifle.

"Attaboy," approved Tom, his own fighting blood fully roused. "They've asked for it—give it them back. I'm with you in this all the way, Axel. Ben Logan is a good pal of mine—we can count on him to back us up."

Another shot cracked out from the kneeling man. It pinged off Haakon's antler, making the deer shy and leap violently. Axel's rifle cracked and the rifleman in the snow gave a cry and dropped his gun. He rolled over, clutching his arm.

The other two with the sled left him there. One of them threw a rifle to his shoulder and fired. The bullet whistled over the toboggan. Axel fired again. The two crooks ducked low . . .

The shots had been heard in the village, only half a mile away now. Men were running out to see what was happening. A three-dog sled was putting out, coming dashing straight for the battlefield, its red-coated driver lashing his team to their best speed. The sun glinted on silver buttons on his coat . . .

"Why," cried Tom, excitedly "this is Ben Logan coming, sure as you're born."

It was indeed the famous Mountie sergeant, who had been issuing trapping licences in Wyatt's Ferry before returning to Eagle Pass.

At the sight of his red uniform all the fight went out of the two hi-jackers—and out of their partner, who was now limping slowly up to the halted dog-sled still clutching his wounded arm.

Sergeant Ben Logan drove up to Axel's toboggan first. He knew Tom Price well, but he had never met Axel.

"What's the shooting about Tom?" he demanded, his eye boring into Axel's. Then he looked at the heaving flanks of the rein deer and finally across the snow to the dog-sled a hundred yards away "What the heck——!" he exclaimed. "Say, if that isn't you malemute team, Tom, my name's not Logan."

"You're dead right, Ben—that's my team and my sled and my cargo. Those three wolf hunters as they called themselves, hi-jacked me yesterday and stole the whole outfit."

"So you hired this caribou taxi and chased right after them?"

"Right again, Ben," grinned Tom. "Say, I want you to meet Axel Thorsen and his king caribou Haakon—the fastest animal on four legs in the North."

"There!" exclaimed Axel in triumph. "You've said it at last Tom."

Ben Logan knew nothing of their deer versus dogs argument which had lasted for years. But he wasn't noticing, anyhow. He was striding away across the snow to the three crooks who were waiting in sullen resignation for his coming.

THE END

ANDY BARCLAY'S DESERT BLUFF

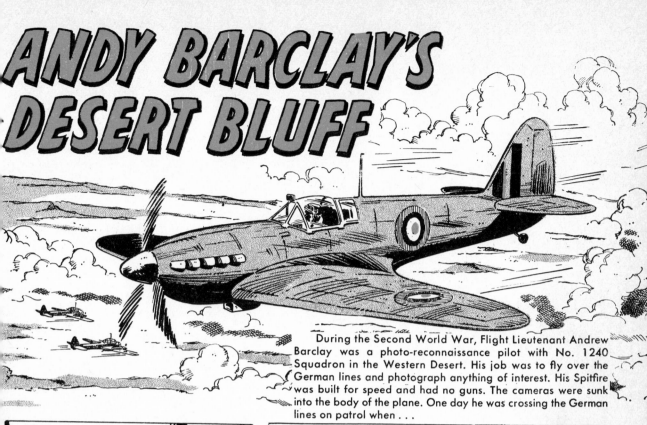

During the Second World War, Flight Lieutenant Andrew Barclay was a photo-reconnaissance pilot with No. 1240 Squadron in the Western Desert. His job was to fly over the German lines and photograph anything of interest. His Spitfire was built for speed and had no guns. The cameras were sunk into the body of the plane. One day he was crossing the German lines on patrol when . . .

RED THREE TO BASE. TWO GERMAN BOMBERS HEADING YOUR WAY. OVER.

ROGER, RED THREE. WE'LL BE WAITING FOR THEM. OUT.

THERE'S NOTHING GOING ON ROUND ABOUT HERE. I'LL TRY GOING A BIT FURTHER SOUTH.

THERE'S SOMETHING DOWN THERE. I'LL GO DOWN AND HAVE A LOOK.

I'D BETTER SWITCH ON THE CAMERAS NOW. THEN I'LL GET ANYTHING THAT HAPPENS TO BE DOWN THERE.

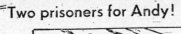

Two prisoners for Andy!

NOW I'LL FIND OUT WHAT REALLY HAPPENED TO THAT JERRY.

THERE IT IS. I WONDER IF ANY OF THE CREW ARE ALIVE. IT HASN'T CAUGHT FIRE SO MAYBE THE PILOT MANAGED TO LAND IT.

THERE DOESN'T SEEM TO BE ANYBODY ALIVE IN THERE. I'D BETTER GO IN AND SEE.

THIS ONE'S STILL ALIVE. THE OTHER IN THERE ISN'T TOO BAD BUT HE'S WOUNDED IN THE ARM. IT MUST HAVE BEEN WHEN THEY WERE ATTACKED BY OUR FIGHTERS BEFORE. I CERTAINLY ONLY HIT IT WITH ONE SHOT AND THAT SEEMS TO HAVE KILLED THE PILOT. THIS BOD HERE MUST HAVE LANDED IT—HE WAS LEANING OVER THE PILOT!

SO YOU'VE COME ROUND. I'VE JUST HAULED YOUR MATE HERE OUT OF THE PLANE BUT HE'S WOUNDED IN THE ARM.

HE WAS WOUNDED BY YOUR FIGHTERS. YOU MUST BE THE PILOT WE SHOT DOWN. BUT YOU MANAGED TO KILL OUR PILOT WITH YOUR REVOLVER. I JUST MANAGED TO LAND THE PLANE AND NO MORE.

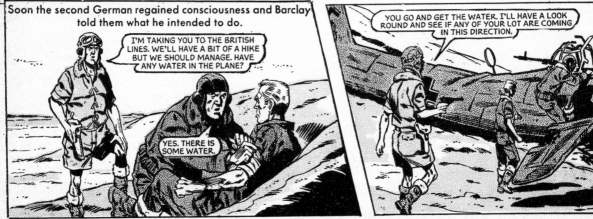

Soon the second German regained consciousness and Barclay told them what he intended to do.

I'M TAKING YOU TO THE BRITISH LINES. WE'LL HAVE A BIT OF A HIKE BUT WE SHOULD MANAGE. HAVE ANY WATER IN THE PLANE?

YES. THERE IS SOME WATER.

YOU GO AND GET THE WATER. I'LL HAVE A LOOK ROUND AND SEE IF ANY OF YOUR LOT ARE COMING IN THIS DIRECTION.

AHA! I THOUGHT THEY MIGHT START NATTERING ONCE I WAS OUT OF THE WAY. I MUST FIND OUT WHAT THEY ARE UP TO.

THIS PILOT MUST NOT GET BACK. HE IS THE ONE WHO SAW A TROOP CONCENTRATION.

JA, JA, I UNDERSTAND. NEVER MIND, WE'LL DEAL WITH HIM. HE HAS ONLY GOT ONE GUN. HE HAS ALREADY USED UP TWO OF THE SIX BULLETS FROM IT. THAT LEAVES FOUR.

THAT'S IT. YOU TWO KEEP IN FRONT OF ME WHERE I CAN KEEP AN EYE ON YOU. AND REMEMBER I'M THE ONLY ONE WHO'S GOT A GUN—I SEARCHED YOU TWO WHILE YOU WERE UNCONSCIOUS!

THAT FIGHTER IS DIVING ON US. HE MUST BE OUT TO MAKE SURE I DON'T GET BACK. RUN FOR THE ROCKS. HE'S GOING TO OPEN FIRE.

HE IS FIRING AT HIS OWN MEN AND HE DOESN'T EVEN CARE.

AYE, HE'S MORE INTERESTED IN STOPPING ME THAN SAVING YOUR LIVES.

HE'S NOT STAYING. HE MUST HAVE JUST BEEN RETURNING FROM A PATROL AND WAS ORDERED TO HAVE A GO AT US. BUT HE'LL BE ABLE TO TELL THE REST OF YOUR LOT WHERE WE ARE. COME ON, WE'D BETTER GET MOVING.

WE MUST REST. WE HAVE BEEN MOVING FOR HOURS NOW AND HANS HERE IS IN A BAD WAY. IF WE DO NOT STOP SOON HE WILL DIE.

ALL RIGHT. THERE'S A WADI AHEAD THERE. WE'LL HAVE A REST IN IT FOR AN HOUR BUT THAT'S ALL.

The three soon reached the wadi and sat down to rest, but Barclay had to stay awake. Then . . .

A SNAKE! I'VE GOT TO KILL IT OR IT'LL GET THAT GERMAN.

—101—

"You could have jumped me any time."

104

The End

HE TEARAWAY OF THE TABLES

I DON'T suppose any of us at the Premier Table Tennis Club will forget that first hectic season with Grierson. From the moment he first slunk into the clubroom to the time he turned up for the vital championship play-off escorted by a squad of brawny policemen, the place was never quite the same. Perhaps it never will be again.

I'm Bill Hicks, by the way, match secretary and captain of Premier A, current First Division champions of the Brigham and District Table Tennis League. But at the time my story begins, when that weird character, Grierson, came into our lives, we had finished up the previous season by narrowly escaping relegation into Division Two.

It was practice night at the clubroom a week or so before the beginning of the new season. Determined to improve upon our lowly position, we had been practising hard throughout the summer.

There were about a dozen of us fighting for four places in each of the A and B teams, so competition was pretty keen.

As you're probably aware, table tennis isn't a game for slow-coaches. It's one of the fastest

> **The table tennis tough with a chip on his shoulder.**

games in the world, and has come a long way from the days of ping-pong on the dining-room table to its present day status as an international sport.

If you haven't played the game, you don't know what you are missing. Players in other sports have found it the ideal game for speeding up the eye and footwork. If you can intercept a table tennis

ball in flight, there's not many other balls will get by you.

But I'm letting my enthusiasm run away with me. On the night in question, first and second-teamers were battling it out on the two match tables while a few newcomers to the club cut their teeth, as it were, on the slower, remaining table.

I was in the middle of a tense three-gamer with Jim Brooks, last season's B number one. Captain or not, as number four in the A team I wasn't sure of a regular berth, and Brooks was laying into me as though to emphasise the fact.

The scores were 21-17, 18-21, and the final game stood at 17 all. Being a defensive player myself, I stood well back from the table while Jim Brooks worked himself up into a frenzy trying to hit me into the street.

He nearly did, too, but I managed to return the ball back, sometimes by the thickness of an eyebrow. Attracted by the " needle " in the match, the other players left their games to come over and watch. Their presence heightened the tension.

Jim fairly plastered one down my backhand wing, but I retrieved it with a vicious chop that sent it back loaded with back-spin. Brooks was a wily bird, however, and retaliated with a cunningly disguised drop-shot that barely crept over the net.

With a desperate bound I leapt in and scrambled it back. The ball reared up and Jim swept in for the "kill." A sixth-sense, born of experience, sent me scurrying back before he could hit the ball into my body, which is the worst place to be caught near the table.

It was one of the unwritten rules of the game not to stand in a position interfering with the free movement of the players, practice match or not. There could have been a nasty accident.

If I expected an apology, I was disappointed.

"Serves you right," glowered the youth, with his lip curling. "The table's over there, not out here."

He jerked a nicotine-stained thumb behind me, and stamped a heavy boot on the remains of his cigarette. I struggled to regain my self-control, a task made even harder by the fact that the blade of my bat had snapped.

"No," said Jim, swallowing hard. "Let's see how big-mouth shapes against a bloke who couldn' hit his way out of a paper bag!"

"Suits me, Mister," said the youth, with all the self confidence in the world. He strolled over to the table wreathed in tobacco smoke.

"Played before?" I grunted.

He gave a slight nod.

I tossed him over one of the club bats. He caught it neatly and examined it closely.

The thickness of the blade seemed to be puzzling him.

"Here," he scowled suspiciously "What's wrong with this bat?"

I explained to him that the ba

Bill's first meeting with Grierson was a disastrous one. They collided in the middle of a game.

I'd judged his move nicely, but whether or not I could have returned the ball I'll never know, because I ran into somebody with a thud and fell in a tangle of arms and legs on to the floor.

I picked myself up dazedly, almost at the same time as a thin, scruffy-looking youth was scrambling to his feet.

For a moment my gaze met a pair of shifty eyes in a sallow, grimy face before the newcomer turned away to look for a dropped cigarette. He wore washed-out jeans and a black, imitation-leather jacket.

Then I lost my temper as my concentration snapped.

"Why the blazes don't you look where you're going?" I snarled.

"Look," I said curtly. "At this club we play how we like. As a defensive player, I stand well back. And I don't expect the playing area to be cluttered up with spectators!"

The youth openly jeered.

"You won't get many spectators the way you play, Mister," he chortled. "Standing back to a bloke that couldn't hit his way out of a paper bag!"

I had to hold back the hot-tempered Jim Brooks from doing the newcomer an injury. Not that the youth seemed bothered. He was too busy lighting another cigarette.

"Come on, Jim," I said, shrugging my shoulders. "Let's finish the game—I've got a spare bat with me."

he was holding was of the "sand wich" variety, one of the two types of face standardised since 1959. Each side of the blade was covered with a layer of cellular rubber and surfaced with an outer layer of standard, pimpled rubber.

This type of bat had more "give" than the traditional pimpled rubber-only face, and was consequently a lot faster in action. Most of the recent world champions favoured the sandwich bat and could achieve fantastic speed and spin with its aid. It was, however, much more difficult to master than the pimpled rubber bat.

Obviously the newcomer had never seen one before, and he listened intently as I described the

Grierson disgraced himself by throwing his bat on the floor when his opponent got a net-cord.

onstruction of the bat to him. I could sense Jim Brooks fidgeting impatiently at the other end of he table.

Hardly any of us at the club ad much use for the sandwich bat, but the fact failed to impress he youth. His one question was straight to the point.

" Then this is the fastest bat, Mister ?" he asked.

I nodded.

" I'll use it," he muttered.

. . . . . .

I sat down in the umpire's chair and watched the two players have a brief warm-up. Straight away, I could see that Grierson, as the youth was called, had played before.

He was awkward, even unorthodox in style, but he seemed to have plenty of time to make his shots—the hallmark of a good player. The new bat was obviously troubling him, and as he insisted on playing in his boots, his footwork was clumsy.

All the same, I had the feeling that Jim Brooks was going to have his hands full as I called out the start of the game. I had to tell Grierson to put out his cigarette.

Grierson served first, and for those who are not familiar with the rules, each player has five consecutive services. The game is played up to twenty-one points unless the score reaches 20-all. After this, each player has one service in turn, the winner being the one who first wins two points more than his opponent.

Within a matter of moments, Grierson was love-5 down. His services with the strange bat were too bad to be true, and not one of them hit the table.

Then it was Brooks' turn. Varying his spin, he served four winners in a row. But his final fast top-spin serve was returned with such speed that he never even saw it !

1-9, and Grierson pulled himself together. Instead of trying to serve outright winners he contented himself with just getting the ball into play. The rallies grew longer, although Jim increased his lead to 13-2 with some vicious backhand flicks.

Grierson retaliated by hitting two looped top-spinners that fairly leapt by the startled Brooks. He then returned the next two services straight into the net, coming into the picture again by crashing in a shot that almost split the ball as it streaked through Jim's defence.

5-15. Grierson was perspiring freely, his curly hair hanging wetly over his narrow forehead. His face was set in a scowl of concentration, and whenever he missed I could hear him muttering to himself. He hit three on in a row and two off.

17-8. Jim serving again. Grierson chortled loudly as he belted in an attacking shot that clipped the net and just dropped over the other side. Jim gritted his teeth at losing the point and returned one of the youth's smashes straight back into his skinny body to make it 18-9.

He hit two more winners out of sheer temper to make it 20-9. But Grierson fought back savagely, hitting like a tiger and never moving more than a pace or two back from the table.

Then it was Jim's turn to get a net-cord. It was a beauty, too, flicking the net and rolling gently over to the other side to win the first game.

Grierson disgraced himself by shouting with temper and throwing his bat down on the floor.

They changed ends for the second game and Grierson opened his account by belting all of Jim's five serves for outright winners.

To this day, I don't think I ever saw anyone hit a ball as hard as this scruffy-looking youth with the long, scrawny arms. They seemed to uncoil like whips as he played his shots.

His most pulverising was the loop. It's played with a looping action that gives top-spin to the ball. Grierson used it in deadly fashion.

In a whizz-bang five minutes a shaken Jim Brooks changed ends for the final game, after losing by the hideous margin of 3-21 ! And there was no mercy in Grierson's beady little eyes as he began to serve in the decider.

I wish I could have stopped the game in a way. Jim hadn't a chance. He pulled out every shot he knew, but the ferret-faced newcomer literally tore him apart.

Forehand and backhand drives, looped top-spin, and drop-shots shattered Jim to a 21-love defeat

Bill Hicks had a visitor one day and what he had to say gave Bill a shock.

that was received by the club in an incredulous silence. And all of us knew, from Tom Hardy our A team number one right down to number four in the B team, that the scowling, shifty Grierson could do the same to any one of us !

I wish I could tell you that things turned out all right after that. But I can't—things never did with Grierson around. Although Jim made a sporting attempt to congratulate him, Grierson shrugged his narrow shoulders and slunk out into the night.

The Truth About Grierson

THE following evening, I was just finishing tea when I received a visit from a tall burly man. As we sat over a cup of tea, he introduced himself as Mr Barlow, Grierson's probation officer!

Evidently the youth had been to report to him after visiting our club last night. Mr Barlow had had the full story out of him and

had been impressed by the interest he showed in the game.

Now, the probation officer wanted to know if I could fix up Grierson as a member of the club.

Grierson was one of Mr Barlow's big problems. He had a juvenile crime record as long as your arm and had spent a great deal of time in various approved schools. That's where he'd picked up his table tennis.

Mind you, he hadn't had much of a start in life. One of a large family, with a weak, easily-led father, he had been fending for himself most of the time.

All the same, it was pretty certain that any further lapse on his part would be rewarded with a prison sentence. Although he seemed to be doing his best to go straight, he had been seen around on occasions with some rather tough characters.

The biggest problem of all was the outsize chip on his shoulder. His surly attitude had involved him in more than his share of fights, and had cost him several jobs. It didn't help when people taunted him about his record either.

Despite all this, I was keen to play a part in the rehabilitation of this eighteen-year-old tough. I've always had a great deal of faith in the character-building qualities of this game of ours. When you're out there alone under the lights, it brings the best out in you.

First of all, I had to take the other club members into my confidence. They were a decent lot, although in his one brief appearance Grierson had done little to win their hearts.

But if table tennis did little else than keep him on the straight and narrow it would be worth it. Normally I wouldn't have mentioned his record to the others, but as this was virtually his last chance I thought they would be more tolerant if they knew all the facts.

I was proud of the way they rallied round. When Grierson made his next appearance at the club his subscription had been paid by a whip-round. One of the lads found him a pair of rubber shoes and the atmosphere was cordiality itself.

He accepted the shoes with a muffled grunt and showed his appreciation by beating the donor, Tom Hardy, 21-5, 21-2 ! But try as we might, we couldn't get more than the odd word out of him, and the gang of thugs who called into the club for him towards the end of the evening made us shudder.

We breathed again when they departed without trouble.

The season was now upon us and Grierson was registered as our A team number one. Tom Hardy moved back to number two, Jim Brooks had made the grade at number three, and I narrowly scraped into the last berth in addition to skippering the team.

There are twelve rubbers in a league match, each one the best of three games. Each player takes part in two singles and two doubles, making a total of eight singles and four doubles in all.

Number one plays the opposing one and two, number two also one and two, number three plays three and four, and number four also plays three and four. For the doubles you divide into two pairs and play against each of the opposing two pairs.

The battle for the top of the league.

A really close match can last the best part of an evening.

Until Grierson burst upon the league scene, Brigham Bombers A were hot favourites for the Division One title for the fifth year running.

They were recruited from the staff of the huge Brigham Aircraft factory on the outskirts of the town. Their line-up included two county players, plus Stuart Handley, an up-and-coming youngster of sixteen who was being confidently tipped as a future international star.

Then there was the scuffle after another match following an uncomplimentary remark about Borstal boys. Grierson finished up with a black eye, but his opponent got the worst of it!

These were only a few of the reasons why Grierson was passed over for the county side. We'd had the police in at the clubroom on several occasions making inquiries about him.

Evidently he had been seen around with a couple of louts who were under suspicion regarding a

As it happened, it turned out to be an anti-climax. At the time of the match a flu epidemic was sweeping the town like wildfire, and both teams turned out minus most of their stars.

Even the hard-bitten Grierson was laid low. The match ended in a tame 6-6 draw, leaving us both neck and neck at the head of the table.

With one match to go to the end of the season, both sides remained undefeated. Everything depended on the return fixture

Whenever Grierson played, there was some sort of trouble and he was always in the thick of it.

But the coming of Grierson altered many things. His ruthless play demolished the opposition, and we won most of our matches by incredible margins.

With the season almost halfway through, not one of his opponents had reached double figures against him. Our team remained unbeaten —as did the Bombers, whom we had yet to meet.

We certainly hit the news— Grierson saw to that! Wherever we played there was some sort of trouble. Like the time when Grierson called an umpire a short-sighted freak, after a debatable decision.

number of petty, local robberies. But there was no proof that he was mixed up in anything, and at least we never missed things from the club.

Grierson was really looking forward to our first clash with the Bombers, which was due to be played in their canteen They. were unbeaten like ourselves, and young Handley was bang . on form.

He had recently been selected for international trials, and Grierson was determined to show the selectors the folly of their ways. The match was eagerly awaited in local circles.

at our club, and excitement was at fever pitch in the town.

Meanwhile, despite our attempts to win him over, Grierson grew more surly and unsociable than ever. But he took the game seriously, even giving up smoking to increase his fitness.

Yet, as soon as his games were over he would slink away into the night with his seedy cronies. In complete contrast, young Handley had made a big name for himself playing for his country.

Already, I had been forced to split up our best doubles combination of Grierson and Tom Hardy before blood was spilt.

Grierson arrived at the club for the big match — to find the police waiting for him.

Tom was one of the most even-tempered players I had ever met, but the acid jeers of his partner whenever Tom missed a shot, brought his temper to boiling point.

I put Tom with Jim Brooks, and paired up with Grierson myself.

The Big Match

THE night of the big match saw our clubroom packed to capacity. Both teams were supposed to be at full strength, but at a quarter past seven, when the match got under way, there was no sign of Grierson.

Tom Hardy had to take on Handley in the first match of the evening, and received a ruthless two-set pounding, 21-5, 21-6.

We looked anxiously at the clock because having already entered Grierson's name at number one on the score sheet, we were not allowed to field a reserve.

Under the rules, Grierson would forfeit his games if he didn't arrive by a quarter to eight. Obviously we couldn't afford to concede four games to a team like the Bombers and hope to win.

Jim Brooks kept our hopes alive by taking a hard-fought three-gamer from the Bombers' third man. I decided to go on next against their number four. I bit my lip when I saw that the clock

showed twenty-five minutes to eight.

During the warm-up before the game I suddenly noticed several blue-uniformed figures around the room. Among them was the burly form of a grave-faced Mr Barlow, the probation officer.

I didn't have to be a fortune-teller to guess that their visit was closely connected with Grierson's absence.

Despite my worries I took the first game 21-19. As we changed ends there was a sudden commotion at the end of the hall. I heard the strident voice of Grierson raised in bitter protest.

As captain and secretary, I had to go over to see what was the matter. In any case the game couldn't go on during the present uproar, and the umpire suspended the game until order was restored.

I found a dishevelled Grierson in the grasp of two burly constables. He was struggling angrily and arguing with Inspector Browning, who I knew as a keen table tennis fan himself. The clock showed exactly a quarter to eight.

"Lemme go, coppers," snarled Grierson. " I ain't done nothing !"

Mr Barlow, the probation officer, turned to me.

" It's no use," he stated bluntly. " Grierson and his two pals tried to break open the safe at Brigham Aircraft tonight. They were after the payroll."

"That's right," said Inspector

Browning. "They might have got away with it, too, if they hadn't squabbled among themselves. They'd already knocked out the watchman, but one of our patrol cars in the district heard the row they were making and went to investigate.

"When they got there," he went on, " Grierson's two cronies were stretched out on the floor alongside the watchman. Grierson was just scrambling through a window and dropped twenty feet to the ground.. We sent out a general alarm, but he got clean away. Then he was foolish enough to head for the club."

"Nuts," hooted Grierson angrily. " I came here to play in the match and beat this inter-nationalist they've been cracking up ! I admit I was with them two crooks, but they had said they had something on my father and blackmailed me into going with 'em !

"Then they slugged the old watchman, and I set about 'em. You can ask 'em when they come round. Now get your rozzers out of the way till after I've sorted out this lot here !"

He jerked his thumb at the nearby Brigham Bombers, who were standing gaping at the scene.

Say what you like, the Bombers were a sporting lot, even if they had nearly lost their week's wage packets.

They tackled the inspector. The

wanted to retain the title against a full-strength side, they argued.

But the inspector shook his head. He wanted Grierson.

But the crowd wanted Grierson, too. They started a slow handclap and began to chant—

"We want Grierson! We want Grierson!"

There could have been a nasty scene, and the inspector had the presence of mind to see it. After a hasty conference with the probation officer he motioned the two policemen to let Grierson go.

Policemen took up positions near the only exit to the clubroom. Other bobbies mingled with the crowd.

I went back to my game convinced that Grierson was telling the truth. Despite the fact that he had been seen at the scene of the crime, he had turned up at the club to face almost certain arrest. I marvelled at his keenness for the game.

It must have affected my play, because I lost the next two games by wide margins. We were down in the match by two rubbers to one.

"You played like a wet hen!" snarled Grierson to me as he went to the table to play the opposing number two. "Never mind messing about. You should have got stuck into him!"

He was right, of course, and knew it.

Grierson's twenty-foot drop seemed to have left him with a rather bad limp, but he didn't let it put him off his game. With his face set in a bleak scowl he tore into his luckless opponent and defeated him 21-6, 21-4.

Two rubbers each! Then Tom Hardy and Jim Brooks went on in the first doubles of the night. They lost hopelessly against the Bombers' third and fourth players, and Jim had to hold Tom back after some sneering jibes by Grierson.

Grierson and I fought out a fast and furious three-gamer with the aircraft side's 1 and 2. In the end we just edged home, but both myself and the opposing number two had little say in the matter. Grierson and Handley hit away like a couple of fighting cats while we just kept our ends going.

Three rubbers apiece. Jim Brooks went on against their number four and was narrowly

At last Grierson got his chance to play Handley — but he had injured his ankle just before the game.

beaten after a tense match. Then Tom played like a hero and squared the match at four-all against the Bombers' second man.

The next rubber was a massacre. Grierson and I against their 3 and 4. By now, Grierson's limp was proving a handicap, but he never complained once. Nor did he let his impending arrest break his concentration.

Now and again he winced as he came down heavily on his injured leg. Whenever I got in his way I received a snarl for my trouble. He hit like a whirlwind to give us the lead in the match by five rubbers to four. The opposing pair staggered off the table like men in a dream.

Jim and Tom were similarly slaughtered against the Bombers' leading pair, 21-5, 21-2!

Level pegging with two rubbers to go, and it was no use aiming for a draw.

This would mean a replay, and we couldn't be sure that our star player would be available in the future, if the police clustered around the room were anything to go by.

Grierson's ankle was swollen

badly and obviously giving him a lot of pain. I decided to go on against their number three to give him as much rest as possible before tackling Handley.

"Get stuck into him," gritted Grierson as I went out into the middle.

I didn't need telling, and after a close, dour affair with a lot of defensive work, I just scraped home to the biggest cheer of the night. At least, we couldn't lose.

"Well played," grinned a delighted Tom, slapping me on the back as I came off.

"Garn," glowered Grierson. "The other bloke wasn't fit to be let out without a nursemaid. You should have done him two-straight!"

Final Game

THE atmosphere was electric as Grierson limped to the table to take on young Handley. Handley looked every inch the well-groomed internationalist.

Our number one was as scruffy

as ever. His big toe poked out through a hole in his shoe and his hair hung over his sallow face.

A brief warm-up, and then the final rubber began.

Grierson served—and Handley hit it clean past him. A cunning side-spin serve received the same fate.

It took all Handley's skill to return the third service. A quick flash from Grierson's bat sent the ball bouncing into the crowd.

You could have heard a pin drop as they fought it out. Neither would fall back on defence, and most of the rallies consisted of tremendous counter hitting. First one and then the other would gain the upper hand.

At 19-19 Grierson slipped while returning a sizzler down his backhand and lost a point. He must have wrenched his injured ankle, because his face was white with pain when he scrambled to his feet.

But, unperturbed as ever, he hit three consecutive winners with loopers to take the first game.

They changed ends. It took Grierson all his time to hobble to the other end. I decided that a tied match was better than having him seriously damage his ankle, and darted across to ask him to pack up the game.

I should have known better.

" Shove off, Mister," he growled, his narrow chest heaving with exertion. " I'll chuck it when I've done this bloke and not before. The cops can wait !"

He scowled across the table at Handley.

But Handley had a ruthless streak in him, too. He began to play on Grierson's damaged leg like a boxer jabbing his left into an opponent's injured eye.

He switched his attack from wing to wing with bewildering speed, mixing it with cunning drop-shots to keep Grierson on the move.

Grierson fought back desperately, getting everything back and matching hit for hit until it was 15-all. By now, he could hardly move his feet and his face was set in a scowling mask of concentration.

It was obvious that he could never go the full distance in a three-gamer, and you could see him pull himself together for a final supreme effort.

He raised his pace and belted everything back at Handley. The young international proved his class by returning the shots with interest.

Eighteen-all. Suddenly, Handley got a net-cord. You could hear Grierson's snarl of disgust all over the club. Then, as so often happens in this unpredictable game of ours, Handley got another.

Grierson howled with pent-up anger and drew a stern rebuke from the umpire. He smacked his bat angrily against his thigh. 18-20 down ! Could this be the breaking point ?

Then, in a cold relentless fury, Grierson cut loose. He pulled back one point with a backhand drive that cracked the ball first bounce clean into the crowd.

He levelled the scores with a forehand smash that left Handley groping at the air.

Twenty-all. Handley got a third net-cord which Grierson managed to scoop back. The internationalist returned it with all the force of a winner.

Close to the table, caught in a cramped position, Grierson flicked his wrist and took the point with a scorching backhand.

Twenty-one - twenty ! The ball flashed between the two players in a blur of white. An edge to Handley—and Grierson lunged heavily forward to scoop it almost off the floor.

Back came the stinging return from Handley, but Grierson jumped in, almost stumbled— and then, with a fantastic looper, smashed the ball clean past Handley for the winner.

The crowd went wild. Even the policemen cheered.

Then all at once it was all over. Inspector Browning came up with the two hefty constables in close attendance. They had to support Grierson, who could now hardly stand.

" Congratulations, Grierson," said the inspector. " I've got some good news for you."

" You mean the other two have confessed ?" I said breathlessly.

" Aye," said the inspector. " We trapped them into it by setting one against the other. It always works when you question them separately. I've just heard the news from the station.

" All the same," he went on, turning to Grierson, " when we've had a doctor look at that leg of yours you'll have to come to the station to answer a few questions. It shouldn't take long."

I shook Grierson's hand.

" Well played," I said. " We'll have you in the international team next season."

" Garn," he scoffed, " I told you I could do him !"

They moved out slowly, the crowd parting for them. Grierson was cheered all the way. At the door he turned. He scowled. Then he gave me the thumbs-up sign.

" You're not such a bad lot of blokes," he said. " I'll be back to lick you into shape for next season !"

THE END

112

WHAT?—WHERE DID HE COME FROM?

LOVAT'S PASSING THE SERGEANT!

THE TENDERFOOT WON!

WELL DONE, SON!

AMAZING! HERE'S YOUR DOLLAR, JIM. WHO IS THAT FELLER ANYWAY?

HE'S A TENDERFOOT WHO JOINED THE WAGON TRAIN BACK EAST. HE CAN'T SHOOT OR RIDE OR DO CHORES, BUT LIKE AH SAID, HE CAN RUN.

Suddenly—

MAJOR! THE SIOUX ARE HOLDING A BIG POW-WOW. LITTLE DOG HAS CALLED ALL THE TRIBES TOGETHER.

WHAT! THIS IS SERIOUS! IT LOOKS AS THOUGH HE INTENDS TO GO ON THE WARPATH.

The major called over Silas Crow, the leader of the wagon train, and explained the situation—

IF THE SIOUX GO ON THE WARPATH, THERE'LL BE MIGHTY BIG TROUBLE ROUND HERE.

WELL, WE'RE PUSHIN' ON AT SUN-UP AND WE'LL BE MILES AWAY IN A WEEK. SO I AIN'T WORRIED, MAJOR.

Next morning—

WE SHOULD REACH POISON CREEK SETTLEMENT IN THREE DAYS. IF I FIND ANY SIGNS OF INJUN TROUBLE, I'LL ADVISE CROW TO HOLD THE TRAIN THERE FOR A SPELL.

ALL RIGHT. GOOD LUCK, JIM!

Everything went well the first day, but on the second—

OH, NO! TRUST LOVAT TO DRIVE OVER THAT ROCK!

THAT DAD-BURNED TENDERFOOT IS NO USE. I WISH I COULD GET RID OF HIM.

YOW! MY FINGER!

That night—

ALL RIGHT—WE'LL MAKE CAMP HERE!

THERE'S SOMETHING WRONG WITH MY HORSES!

MORE O' THEM ARE KEELIN' OVER! THIS IS MIGHTY SERIOUS!

AND MINE!

Hours later—

AH WISH AH KNEW WHAT WAS WRONG WITH YOU, OLD FELLER. AH'VE TRIED EVERYTHING TO HELP YOU, BUT NOTHING SEEMS TO WORK.

WHAT'S THAT YOU'VE GOT THERE, YOUNG 'UN?

GLAUBERS SALTS! IT'S KIND OF COOLING AND REDUCES FEVER IN HUMANS, SO I THOUGHT IT MIGHT HELP THE HORSES!

AH'LL TRY ANYTHIN'! HERE YOU ARE, BOY!

115

A short while later—

GOSH! IT SURE WORKS, LOVAT—WE'D BETTER TREAT THE REST OF THE HORSES.

BUT THAT'S ALL THE SALTS I HAD!

Jim told Silas Crow about the treatment.

SO, AH RECKON LOVAT AND ME SHOULD SET OUT FOR POISON CREEK ON FOOT AND BUY SOME MORE SALTS AND MAYBE HIRE SOME HORSES. MY HORSE IS BETTER, BUT STILL NOT ENOUGH FOR ME TO RIDE IT.

I SUPPOSE WE'VE NO CHOICE—BUT I JUST HOPE THAT TENDERFOOT DOESN'T MESS THINGS UP.

WE'VE GOT ABOUT TWELVE MILES TO GO, SON, SO LET'S STEP OUT.

SURE THING, JIM!

A couple of miles farther on—

AH WANT YOU TO GO ON, SON, AND GET THE SALTS AND HORSES. AH'M GOIN' TO SCOUT THAT RIDGE FOR SIGN OF SIOUX.

SO THAT'S WHY YOU WANTED ME ALONG! ALL RIGHT, JIM, I'LL BE BACK AS SOON AS I CAN!

Soon—

THERE'S POISON CREEK. IT DIDN'T TAKE ME LONG TO RUN HERE.

Lovat told his story—

WELL, HERE'S YOUR SALTS, SON, BUT I DON'T THINK YOU'LL GET ANY HORSES IN THIS TOWN.

WHY NOT?

NOBODY WILL HIRE ANY HORSES OUT TO YOU IN CASE THEY CATCH THE SAME DISEASE. BUT I PROMISE I'LL SEE THAT YOUR SALTS ARE DELIVERED NEAR YOUR CAMP!

Lovat had to be satisfied with the sheriff's promise.

I'D BETTER GET BACK TO THE TRAIN. I RECKON SILAS CROW WON'T BE TOO HAPPY THOUGH!

116

Jim and Lovat were tied up and led to the Indians' camp.

118

"They're trying to cut me off."

119

When Lovat got to the fort, he told Major Rudd what had happened and the Major was able to take Little Dog and his men by surprise and put an end to the uprising.

THE BARGE THAT WENT TO WAR

During World War One, Skipper Driscoll and Nobby Clark, two English bargees who had been called up into the Army, found an English barge on a Belgian canal. They and the barge were made part of the new Inland Waterway Corps and were placed under the command of Major "Potty" Potter. Their job was to transport men and materials, using the rivers and canals of France and Belgium. They were now in Marseilles to pick up supplies.

Five minutes of fearful destruction!

THEY'VE GOT THE RANGE NOW.

THIS WAY, MESSIEURS. VITÉ! VITÉ!

IN THERE, MAJOR— QUICK!

GAD! THIS IS TOO MUCH! SOMETHING MUST BE DONE!

OUI, BUT WHAT, MONSIEUR? BY THE TIME OUR DEFENCES OPEN FIRE, THE U-BOAT WILL HAVE SUBMERGED!

The Frenchman was right. In five short minutes, the U-boat pumped twenty shells into the harbour and, as the defences swung into action, she submerged and slipped away unscathed.

I'VE NEVER SEEN SO MUCH DAMAGE DONE IN SUCH A SHORT TIME. BUT OF COURSE THEY HAVE A WONDERFUL TARGET HERE—

OUI, AND THEY DO NOT CONFINE THEMSELVES TO THE PORT, MONSIEUR. THEY HAVE SHELLED US BEFORE AND SOMETIMES THEY EVEN ATTACK OUR SHIPPING AS IT ARRIVES. THEY HAVE SUNK SHIPS RIGHT INSIDE THE HARBOUR!

OH! THEY HAVE, HAVE THEY? WELL THAT MIGHT BE A DIFFERENT MATTER. I MUST THINK IT OVER.

Later—

HE'S BEEN AT IT FOR HOURS, SKIPPER. WHAT D'YOU THINK HE'S UP TO?

I DUNNO, NOBBY, BUT KNOWING HIM I RECKON IT SPELLS TROUBLE FOR YOU AND ME, MATE!

IT SEEMS A WASTE OF TIME HANGING ABOUT HERE DOING NOTHING, CHAPS. I'VE DECIDED TO TAKE ON A CARGO OF TIMBER.

GOOD IDEA, SIR. TIMBER IS ALWAYS IN DEMAND AT THE FRONT.

THANK GOODNESS FOR THAT. I WAS BEGINNING TO THINK HE WAS COOKING UP SOME BARMY PLAN FOR TACKLING THAT U-BOAT. IT'D BE JUST LIKE HIM!

Soon—

BY GEORGE, MAJOR, WE'RE PACKING IN THE TIMBER PRETTY TIGHTLY. WE'LL BE LIKE A HUGE, FLOATING BAULK OF WOOD BY THE TIME WE'RE THROUGH LOADING.

ER—YES—I RATHER HOPE WE SHALL, DRISCOLL. THAT WAS MORE OR LESS WHAT I HAD IN MIND.

WE'RE JUST ABOUT FULL, NOW, MAJOR—EXCEPT FOR UP IN THE BOWS. WE COULD GET SOME MORE IN THERE.

OH, NO—NOT THERE, DRISCOLL. WE MUST KEEP THAT SPACE FREE FOR THE GUN!

GUN? YOU MEAN? OH, NO!

THIS NATTY LITTLE FRENCH FIELD GUN OUGHT TO DO THE TRICK NICELY.

BUT WE'LL BE SUNK, MAJOR! ONE SHOT WILL BLOW THIS TUB TO BITS!

OH, I DON'T THINK SO, CHAPS. YOU SEE WE'RE PACKED SOLID WITH WOOD—AND WOOD FLOATS.

THIS WILL DO VERY NICELY. ALL WE HAVE TO DO NOW IS WAIT FOR THE GERMANS TO SHOW UP.

The major hadn't long to wait. Three days later, the U-boat was back again in search of more victims.

ACH! A SUPPLY-BARGE ANCHORED IN THE HARBOUR! SHE IS OF SHALLOW DRAUGHT SO WE WILL NOT USE TORPEDOES. BLOW TANKS! PREPARE TO SURFACE!

GUN-CREW! PREPARE FOR SURFACE ACTION!

Aboard the barge—

THERE SHE IS! NOW FOR IT!

NO—NO! NOT YET, DRISCOLL, WE MIGHT SCARE HER OFF! WE MUST HAVE PATIENCE!

FIRE!

A HIT! ONE MORE SHOT SHOULD DO IT!

MAID OF KENNET

NO EFFECT. WE MUST CLOSE RANGE! HALF-SPEED AHEAD BOTH ENGINES!

The deadly decoy!

125

Guns of this size were made in the late fifteenth century and had to be pulled by great numbers of horses, oxen or men. With a large calibre, they could fire a cannon ball weighing 1,000 lb. over a mile.

A ROUND OF

Large mortars of this type were made during the American Civil War. Mounted on large railway flat-cars, they could be moved from point to point to fire their huge bombs.